FORGOTTEN WATERS

A RICK WATERS NOVEL

CARIBBEAN ADVENTURE SERIES
BOOK TWENTY-ONE

ERIC CHANCE STONE

PUBLISHING

FORGOTTEN WATERS

CHAPTER
ONE

A school of jacks broke the surface and scattered baitfish in all directions as Rick passed the center channel marker exiting the jetties outside of Destin Harbor. Chief's crest was raised, and he jumped up and down, mimicking Choco, who was also excited about being out on the boat. Jules stood on the bow with her camera ready to catch a dolphin in the bow waves. She kept looking back at Rick, who was behind the wheel on the flybridge, laughing when she saw Chief's head pop up and then disappear again. They were all excited to be heading back to Apalachicola. The area was known as the Forgotten Coast and had a mysterious vibe.

Rick always felt a connection to Apalachicola, St. George Island, and the small town of East Port. The area still had a small-town feel, and the locals were friendly. However, this was no pleasure cruise. Sure, they would get some vacation-like time, but the trip was serious. Rick and Jules had taken a day trip in Rick's Bronco to Apalachicola, and Rick noticed a missing persons sign on a telephone pole near the Oyster City

Brewing Company. He still kept a photo of the sign on his iPhone and looked at it often.

Missing Since Oct 20thCindy Richmond22 years old

Last seen at Oyster City Brewing Company$80,000 reward for information leading to her return.

Cindy was a small, fiery brunette who always wore her long hair in a ponytail. She was a certified brewmaster. One night, she vanished into thin air. Her father had not received a ransom demand, but he was getting some threatening emails and phone calls, and a truck had been stalking his property. Rick agreed to help him. They had a meeting scheduled in a couple of days from now, and Jake, Cindy's father, had saved Rick's number in his phone to call if the kidnappers contacted him again. Rick had his phone sitting right in front of him, synced to his Bose headphones. He was listening to all of Cake's albums as he steered the boat down the East Coast. He loved Cake. They had an odd lead singer who spoke and sang, but the band was so tight and their melodies so intricate that they struck a nerve with Rick.

Jules gave up on dolphins and returned to the flybridge.

"Hi, baby, no dolphins, huh?" Rick asked as he pulled off his headphones.

"Nah, that's okay. I'll see some soon, hopefully. How long until we reach Apalachicola?"

Rick glanced at the chart plotter.

"About four hours at this speed. We could go faster, but this is the sweet spot for best fuel efficiency," said Rick.

"We ain't in no hurry. Are you okay up here alone? I wanna finish the Dawn Lee McKenna book I started. I'm gonna read down below," said Jules.

"Oh, yeah, I'm good. Just jamming to some Cake."

"Yuck, the only cake I like is chocolate," Jules said playfully as she kissed Rick on the cheek and headed down below.

Every time Rick played Cake in the Bronco, she inevitably asked him to turn it down. She was not a fan. Rick didn't mind. He wasn't fond of some of the music she liked either. She had gotten into a band from Canada called The Tragically Hip, or just The Hip, as locals called them. Rick appreciated their songs but couldn't get into them as much as he tried. The only song he really dug by them was "New Orleans Is Sinking." He wasn't sure if it was the groove of the song or the fact that he had such a strong connection to New Orleans. He grew up a little over three hours away from New Orleans and visited it more times than he could remember.

As he motored down the coast, he saw all the bait fish breaking the surface and wished for a minute that he were in Nine-Tenths, his 55-foot Viking sport fisher, so he could troll. But he knew they needed to be in the new catamaran, which he named Jules Down Under. He took ownership of the Australian-built treasure-finding vessel after solving a case involving the murder of an oilman from Texas. The boat was highly advanced and had massive tubes on the stern called prop wash diverters. They were used to blow sand on the sea floor to help find treasure beneath the sand. In addition to the fun tubes, as Rick called them, the boat had the most up-to-date side-scanning sonar and every other gadget a treasure finder would ever need. Most people used the term "treasure hunter," but Possum and Rick always said "treasure finder" because they found treasure rather than hunted for it.

The ride was smooth, and the Gulf was calm, with gentle, slow-moving swells that subtly rocked the boat, much like a mother would rock her baby to sleep. Birds gathered over the bait fish, diving into the glassy surface of the water. It was a perfect day to be out on the Gulf.

Choco curled up in the corner and lost interest in searching for birds. He was the lead dog on Rick's dogsled team during a case in Alaska. They bonded so closely that when the case ended, Choco came home with Rick. Chief, on the other hand, only thought he was a dog. He was a rescue cockatoo Rick had gotten from a guy who took a job overseas and couldn't take Chief with him. Clearly, Chief had been raised around dogs. He made three distinct dog sounds: one that sounded like a big barking dog, similar to a hound with a loud woof-woof; a small yip, like a little football dog, which Rick called a yip—most likely a Peekapoo or Pekingese; and a howl like a Beagle. His favorite thing to do was laugh and imitate seagulls.

As they passed Panama City Beach, Rick saw people all along the shoreline. The Florida Panhandle had a different peak season than South Florida. Its busy season is during the summer. However, because of population growth, the seasons are no longer as clearly defined as they once were, meaning traffic is heavy year-round now. Rick could have made better time if he had gone a little further offshore, but he enjoyed hugging the coast. There was something calming about seeing land even when offshore. Rick pulled out his binoculars and scanned several miles around for boat traffic, then set the autopilot and went below to make a sandwich and check on Jules. When he got below deck, Jules surprised him with boudin-stuffed kolaches she had picked up at Buc-ee's and frozen. She knew Rick would be coming down soon because she kept track of his fasting schedule. She knew he had last eaten at 4:00 p.m. the previous day and had heated the kolaches for him.

"Oh my God, kolaches! I love you!" exclaimed Rick.

"I also made you a Live It Up Super Greens Powder drink with creatine. If you're gonna eat bad food, you're also gonna drink something good, Mister," said Jules.

"Yes, ma'am," Rick replied, taking his drink and kolaches back up to the helm.

Rick loved kolaches. He was first introduced to them while living in Texas. He had moved to Florida earlier, before they became widely known, or at least not to Rick. When he returned to Texas after losing his seniority with Northwest Airlines, he became a top private detective and began to see kolaches everywhere. They certainly weren't healthy; puffy dough filled with sausage links or boudin were the two most popular savory types. Others had fruit fillings for the sweet tooths out there.

Once they passed Mexico Beach, Rick was reminded of the song of the same name by his buddy Don Middlebrook. He had met Don at Lulu's in Destin when Don booked a group of trop rock musicians for a benefit for the folks affected by Hurricane Michael. Rick played the song on his iPhone, blasting it through the boat's impressive sound system. He raised his glass of green juice and toasted Don, wondering where he was performing that week. He knew Don lived in Michigan but played all across the country.

They weren't pressed for time, so Rick decided to stop at Saint Joseph Bay and drop anchor near Port Saint Joe. Rick wanted to show Jules a cool restaurant he had visited before. Saint Joseph Bay is a natural harbor with good holding ground for an anchor. He's not big into raw oysters anymore, but they had some amazing baked oysters with bacon, cheddar, scallions, feta, and garlic butter. A couple of kolaches hadn't satisfied his hunger, and he was pretty sure Jules hadn't tried a low country boil, a dish that The Shipwreck Raw Bar excelled at. He had stopped there a few years back, mainly because he liked the restaurant's name, and he was pleasantly surprised at how good the food was and how friendly the staff had been.

They left the boat and headed toward dry land. Jules pulled the dinghy ashore and tossed two lifejackets into it as Rick locked everything up. He wasn't sure, but he had a good idea that the place was pet-friendly, and he carried Chief over to Jules and handed him to her. Choco jumped into the dinghy, eager to go. It was a nice, calm day with almost no waves on the beach. Rick just motored up to the shore and pulled the dinghy onto the sand. There were no docks there because The Shipwreck Raw Bar was just past St. Joseph's Point and directly on the beach with no protection from the open Gulf. They were lucky it was such a calm day; otherwise, he would've had to motor over to the city marina in Port Saint Joe and take an Uber to the restaurant. Since the Gulf was nearly glassy, the beach entrance was right in front of the restaurant.

After Rick secured the dinghy with an anchor in the sand, they walked up the beach toward Highway 98 and entered the restaurant. It was still a little early for lunch, and only a few tables had been seated.

"Hi, are we allowed to bring our pets inside?" Rick asked the bartender.

"Sure, honey, the more the merrier. Oh my God. Isn't he precious?" she said as she spotted Chief.

Rick and Jules found a table along the far-right side wall. The place had an old Florida vibe with laminated tables and beach murals on the walls. It felt like coming home. A couple of local old-timers were already sitting at the bar, several beers in before 11:00 a.m.

"What's his name?" asked the young waitress.

"This is Chief. He thinks he's a dog, and this is Choco. He

thinks he's human, but it's okay—I identify as a boat captain, though I'm actually a private detective," Rick replied, jokingly.

"Can I pet him?" she asked.

"He'll be your best friend if you give him a cracker or a grape," said Rick.

She held up a finger and jogged into the kitchen. She returned with a small basket of crackers, peeled the wrapper off a saltine, and held it toward Chief. Chief took it in his beak, then held it out with his foot and nibbled on it.

"Oh my God, he's holding it like a human," she said as she snapped a few photos with her phone.

"I'm so sorry, can I get y'all something to drink before you order?"

"No worries. He does that to everyone. No matter where I take him, he acts like he's the boss. I think he knows he's adorable, too. I'll get an ice water. Jules?"

"I'll take a water with lemon and a Diet Coke."

"Coming up."

"Any specials, or just what's on the menu?" asked Jules.

"We have gator bites today. They are kinda like chicken strips, only alligator."

"You wanna try them, Jules?"

"When Rome," she replied.

"You mean when in Rome?"

"Huh?"

"Never mind. Yes, we'll have an order of those first," said Rick.

The waitress brought out the drinks, a small bowl of water for Chief, and a dog bowl of water for Choco.

"Thank you so much. That was thoughtful," said Jules.

"I'm gonna wash my hands real quick."

Rick walked over to the restroom and stepped inside. He

washed his hands and saw the poster of the missing girl in the mirror behind him. The reward had increased to $200,000.

Damn.

He snapped a picture of it and headed back to the table.

"Look, Jules. It's up to 200k now."

"Wow. What time is your meeting with her father?"

"We're meeting him tomorrow after lunch. He's gonna text me, which reminds me. Do you wanna sleep on the boat or get a hotel? We never discussed it."

"Either way, we can play it by ear. Is there a place to dock and plug in?"

"Yeah, Scipio Creek Marina has transient slips. It's a great location. We can start there and see how it is," said Rick.

"Sounds like a plan."

"They have a great restaurant there too, called Half Shell Dockside. I won a bingo game there one night. Maybe we can play one night."

"Cool. I love bingo," said Jules.

The waitress dropped off the gator bites.

"Do y'all know what else you are gonna order?"

"Yeah, we'll get an order of the St. Joe Beached Oysters and the Low Country Boil."

"Great choice. We got some nice Royal Red Shrimp in today."

"Oh yeah, boyeee!!!" exclaimed Rick.

Jules didn't like the gator bites, so Rick ate most of them. She tried to avoid fried food and often encouraged Rick to do the same. Rick loved fried fish but had eaten more blackened fish since meeting Jules than ever before in his life. He appreciated her efforts to keep him healthy and rarely argued with her —except when it came to cheese sticks. There was no other way to make them, and he loved them. He fell in love with them when he was a kid. He had them at a TGIF's with his parents and was hooked ever since.

They both loved the oysters and the Low Country boil. After dinner, Jules ordered a piece of key lime pie and two forks. As they waited for dessert, Rick's phone whistled. He looked down and saw it was a text from Jake, the missing girl's father. He asked Rick if there was any way he could meet him sooner than the next day. Rick texted back:

We're two hours out. Where can we meet?

Jake texted Rick an address. Rick popped it into his phone and saw it was a beach house on St. George Island.

"We're gonna need a car or use Uber, Jules. Jake wants to meet us this afternoon."

Jules usually took care of all the reservations and pulled out her phone. "Wow, there are no car rental companies, except for Turo, but there is Uber and Lyft."

"Okay, we can grab an Uber today. Possum said he wants to bring the motorhome over to help with the case. I'll have him tow the Bronco over, and he and Malia can stay in the RV unless we need to rent a house or something to have a war room."

"Good plan. I'll pay the bill with the company card," said Jules.

Rick thanked the waitress and the bartender, then took Choco outside to do his business. Jules came out shortly after, and they all headed back to the dinghy. Once on the catamaran, Jules tied the dinghy to the stern, and Rick pushed the throttles forward. Since it was such a calm day, Rick decided to go a little farther offshore to avoid the navigation channel so he could make better time. Staying in the channel would take close to two and a half hours, but outside, they made it in under two hours.

They pulled into the marina and were met by the manager.

"Howdy, can we get a transient slip with electric and water?"

"Yes, sir, it's three dollars a foot plus twenty-five dollars for electricity and water."

"Sold!" exclaimed Rick.

Rick side-tied the catamaran near the restaurant entrance, got off, and shook hands with the marina manager. They completed the paperwork, and Jules placed Chief in his travel cage and Choco in his sleeping kennel. She set the air conditioner to a comfortable temperature and filled their bowls with water and food.

"You two be good. We'll be back before you know it," said Jules.

Rick returned to the boat and told Jules the Uber would arrive in six minutes.

"I talked to Possum, and he's coming over in the morning in the motorhome. He said there's a cheap dry camp park under the bridge over to Eastpoint, and he's gonna look to see if there are any other spots. You ready?"

"Yep, let me grab my backpack, and let's roll," said Jules.

A man in a Jeep Grand Wagoneer pulled up with his window down.

"Rick?"

"Yep, thanks."

They both climbed into the back seat, and the driver took off, headed for St. George Island.

"I see you're going to Jake Richmond's place. That's terrible what happened to his daughter. I saw on Facebook that she is still missing."

"Yeah, do you know her?" asked Rick.

"Everyone knows Jake and Cindy. They are well known

here. Cindy is just a sweetheart. I sure hope it all turns out okay for her. I'm praying," said the driver.

Rick saw his name was Carlos on the Uber app.

"Thanks, Carlos. I don't know how long we'll be. Will I get you again if I use the app?"

"It's a crap shoot if you use the app. Here, take my card. I can come back and pick you up myself if you'd like. You can just pay via PayPal or Cash App."

"Thanks a lot, Carlos," said Rick as they arrived.

"Give my best to Jake. Tell him we're all praying for Cindy."

"Will do, Carlos. Thanks for the lift."

Rick closed out the app and tipped Carlos ten bucks.

Rick and Jules approached the huge beach house. It was beautiful—bright yellow with sharp white trim and a full wraparound porch. Rick always wanted a house like that, with a big porch all around. They went upstairs, and before they could ring the doorbell, Jake Richmond stepped outside to greet them.

"Glad y'all could make it. Who is this pretty girl?" asked Jake.

"Hi, Jake. This is Jules, my wife. She's one hell of an investigator and bail enforcement agent."

"You are a bounty hunter?" asked Jake.

"Well, that's the old school name for it. Now they call it bail enforcement officer or recovery agent. But I'm old school, so yes, I'm a bounty hunter," said Jules.

"I like this girl. Y'all come in."

Jake led them to his study in the beach house. His cheerful mood shifted when they started talking about Cindy. His eyes filled with tears, and he became emotional. It was obvious to Rick and Jules how deeply he cared for his daughter.

"What's the latest with the phone calls, emails, and what-not?" asked Rick.

"Let me show you. They are freaking vague. Here's the latest one. I can forward all of them to you."

Jake opened his laptop and spun it around. Rick and Jules read the email.

From: CJ Cooper <CJCoop212976@gmail.com>
To: Jake Richmond <Jake_Richmond_1961@gmail.com>
Date: Thu, Nov 13, 2025, 4:55 p.m.

Subject: (Cindy)

Your daughter is alive and well for now. You know what you have to do. Do the right thing, and she will be released. Stay greedy, and she will be sacrificed. Don't build any more for the sake of our ancestors.

CJ.

"That is vague. What are they referring to when they talk about you building?"

"I have no plans at the moment. I have developed several properties here on the island and own a large piece of land on the east end that I have considered developing, but most likely won't. It is valuable land, but my daughter and I go camping out there sometimes, and I really don't have the heart to develop it."

Rick read and re-read the email several times and pondered a bit.

"Do you think it could be natives? What indigenous tribes are in the area?" asked Rick.

"Indians? Why do you think Indians?" asked Jake.

"The wording. I keyed in on the words 'sacrifice' and 'ancestors.'"

"Wow, I can see I picked the right private investigator. The land was once home to the Muscogee Creek and Apalachee tribes and later the Seminole. I do know that the Apalachee tribes used the island as a trade hub. My daughter and I found a few points out there. By points, I mean arrowheads."

"I'm very aware of points. My partner, Possum, taught me about them. He'll be here tomorrow, which reminds me—can you recommend a good campground nearby? We have a 44' Entegra Aspire motorcoach he's coming over in. He was planning to dry camp by the bridge at Battery Park for a few days if need be," said Rick.

"Oh, nonsense. Here."

Jake opened the drawer in his desk and tossed Rick a set of keys.

"This is for the new house I just finished. I just got the CO from the state, and I haven't listed it on Airbnb yet. I have ten of them on the island. This one has a fifty-foot cement pad beside it with full hookups. Y'all can stay in the house and use the pad as long as you need. I insist. You came in your boat, right?"

"Yeah, we're docked in a transient slip over at Scipio Creek Marina," said Rick.

"Bring your boat over. There's a massive dock with electric and water. Plus, the house is on the edge of the property we talked about. I'm not sure that's what they are referring to in the email, but you can see it from the house's window. Feel free to scout around out there, treasure hunt, whatever. You have my full permission," said Jake.

Jake's phone rang, and he held up his finger and took the call.

"Okay, I'll be right over," he said. "Rick, I have to cut this short. Can we meet again over dinner at the new house? I have to put out some fires. I'll have it catered for the four of us. 7:00

okay? The address is on the keychain. Feel free to use any of the toys. Just fill them with gas when you're done."

"Wow, thanks. We can do that. I'll call an Uber to head back to the boat."

"I'll give you a ride. I gotta run into town now."

"Perfect."

Jake drove Rick and Jules back to the marina and took off quickly. Rick settled the bill with the dock master and set the chart plotter for the house on the bay on St. George Island. He texted Possum the address and told him he wouldn't have to do any dry camping.

CHAPTER
TWO

Rick motored across the glassy Apalachicola Bay, passed under the bridge, and headed south to Rattlesnake Cove. The house sat on the point and was absolutely beautiful. It was a peach color with soft accents. On the roof was a widow's walk with views of both the bay and the Gulf.

Rick slowly pulled up to the dock, and Choco jumped off, running to the backyard to roll around like a madman in the grass.

Crazy dog.

Rick tied the bow while Jules took care of the stern and spring lines. They unloaded the boat and carried all their belongings into the house, including Choco's sleep kennel and Chief's travel cage. The back porch was fully screened in and the perfect spot for the pets to hang out. With a grill smoker just outside the screen door, Rick planned to spend a lot of time out there himself. The long dock ended where the cement pad for the motorhome began. The house was designed with toys in mind. Besides the long dock for his boat, there was a twenty-four-foot Scout 240 XSF center console with a 300 HP Yamaha and a swim platform on a lift in front of a gorgeous fish cleaning station. There were four jet skis on lifts beside that. Rick had to keep reminding himself that he was there to work, not play.

Rick set up Chief's portable PVC perch on the porch and gave him some grapes. Jules grabbed Rick by the arm and nearly ran as she pulled him upstairs.

"You gotta see this!"

The master bedroom had a full view of the bay in the back and the Gulf in the front. It took up the entire third floor. There was a his-and-hers walk-in closet on each side of the bedroom, a cold-water plunge, a separate rain shower room, and a full hot tub.

"Holy shit! This is not a beach house. It's a freaking mansion," said Rick.

"I know. I almost feel guilty staying here. We're here to find a missing girl and not take a holiday," said Jules.

"I thought the same thing earlier. Let's think about it this way: if we are relaxed, comfortable, and refreshed, we can think more clearly and hopefully make better progress than if we were camping out on the boat."

"I guess that makes sense," agreed Jules. "We could debate it until we're blue in the face, but it is what it is."

"Blue in the face," replied Rick.

"Huh?"

"Never mind. Oh, I got a text from Possum, and he decided to head here earlier. They'll be here in a couple of hours. Hot tub?"

Jules found some aromatherapy beads for the hot tub and filled it up. The look in her eyes told Rick she had more on her mind than just soaking in the hot tub, and he was happy to oblige. Rick climbed in, and she gently massaged his shoulder and kissed his neck. It was a sweet start to a happy ending. They made love in the tub and afterward on the four-poster bed. Rick had never felt more relaxed, and they both drifted off to sleep until Chief came strolling in from his climb down off his perch and sat on Rick's chest, tugging at his chest hair.

"You little bugger, how'd you get in here? You better not have chewed up anything in the house."

Rick felt the bed shift and saw Choco lying at the foot of it as if he belonged there.

"Okay, you two Houdinis, back to the cages."

Rick threw on his shorts and carried Chief down the stairs to the porch. Chief had managed to climb down from his perch and up the stairs to the third floor. He wasn't sure how Choco got his cage handle open, but he was starting to wonder if Chief let him out. Rick was pretty sure there was no cage on the planet that Chief couldn't escape from eventually, given enough time. After he fed and watered them again, he checked his watch and realized he had been asleep for an hour and a half.

"Shit, Possum will be here soon. Thank you, Chief, for being my alarm clock."

Rick climbed upstairs and rustled Jules from her slumber.

"We need to get ready; Possum and Malia will be here soon."

"Crap, wow. We really slept, didn't we?"

"Yep, thank goodness Chief came up and woke me up. Choco too."

"Damn, I slept right through it."

"You must've needed it, baby."

Rick rinsed off under the rain shower to wash the Essence

of Paradise bath beads from his skin, then got dressed. Jules went right after him, threw on a sundress, and put away all the clothes from the suitcases. She always did that.

Rick climbed up the last stairwell to the roof to check out the widow's walk.

"Jules, you gotta come look!" hollered Rick.

The sun was setting over the Gulf, and the view from the rooftop was spectacular. Small flocks of pelicans flew in V formations just above the water as sandpipers did their back-and-forth dance with the waves, searching for snails and other treats to eat.

"Jules, you see those pelicans flying just above the water in formation?"

"Yeah."

"You see how one side of the V's is longer than the other side? You know why?"

"Why?"

"Because there's more pelicans on one side," replied Rick with a grin.

"Shut up!" said Jules as she playfully slapped his arm. "It is beautiful up here."

"I agree. It truly is. Oh, look, Possum is coming up the road."

Rick quickly texted Possum:

Park and come in the back door; climb up all the stairs to the widow's walk. You can catch the sunset.

10-4!

Within minutes, Possum and Malia reached the roof.

"Wow, this place is amazing!" exclaimed Possum.

Possum had a little cooler with him.

"I came prepared."

He handed Rick and Jules each a can of Athletic Free Wave

non-alcoholic IPAs and cracked open two Buds for himself and Malia. They clinked cans together and made a toast to Jesus for giving them such a perfect sunset. Rick did the same joke about the pelicans for Malia. Possum had heard all of Rick's jokes and even egged him on as he pointed at the small cemetery on the empty lot next to the house.

"Look, Rick, a local cemetery," said Possum with a wink.

Rick grinned back,

"Malia, did you know that local folks who live around here aren't allowed to be buried here?"

"Why not?"

"They have to be dead first," said Rick.

"Oh my God. You are too crazy!" exclaimed Malia.

Possum met Malia on the Big Island in Hawaii while they were working on a case. They were a perfect match. She was working as a house manager for the man who had hired Rick for the case. Not long after the case ended, she quit that job. She needed a change, and Possum was exactly what she was looking for. She was an excellent surfer, and the local waves were her only complaint about the Panhandle. She had saved a lot of money from her years working for the billionaire in Hawaii, and she received a severance gift when she moved on. She trained her successor well, and her boss was pleased with the girl she promoted to take her place. She wasn't hurting for money. She and Possum would visit Hawaii so she could surf, and they even went to Tahiti a few times. Possum was content to sit on the beach and photograph and video her with his long lens on his Canon M-50. Rick hadn't seen Possum so happy in years. He deserved it.

"Well, kids. Pick a floor. You can choose either the first or the second. There are three bedrooms on each floor. I need to talk to Gary and see if he and Kelly will be able to make it. I know Clay finishes his 737-flight course soon, so I have no idea what Gary's planning. I'll give him a call after we meet with Jake again over dinner. He said he's catering it here and will be here around 7:30 p.m., so we have a little time before he arrives. I can unhook the Bronco from the motorhome while you and Malia get situated unless you want to stay on the bus?" asked Rick.

"Nah, we'll stay in the house. I think we'll take a room on the first floor. We can use the third bedroom, which looks like a study, for the war room. It will be more productive for us to be in the house."

"Smart thinking, Possum. You got those Bronco keys?"

"They're hanging in the first cabinet when you walk inside the motorhome to the left."

"Gotcha. I'll take care of it," said Rick.

Rick grabbed the keys and unhooked the Bronco from the Blue Ox towing system, then put the transfer case back into two-wheel drive. He backed out and parked in the circular drive in front of the house. He noticed the garage and walked over. The side door was open. He thought maybe he'd park the Bronco inside instead until he opened the door and stepped inside.

It was a long three-car garage. Inside, there were four Can-Am side-by-sides and four Yamaha YZ 125 motocross bikes. Rick was immediately drawn to the motocross bikes. He had raced motocross back in his high school days and drove a similar one back in the day. It had been a few years, but he thought he'd give it a try and show off a little. He pushed the button to open the garage door, threw on a helmet, and fired up the 125s. He texted Jules to tell everyone to come out to the front door, then took off down the road.

We're out front; where are you?

Rick came roaring down the street, doing a wheelie. It didn't take him long to get back into the groove. The newer Yamaha YZ 125s seemed lighter. It had been over thirty years since he last raced, so technology had surely made for a better bike. Rick passed the house, turned around, and did another wheelie going the other way. It was starting to get too dark and dangerous, so he whipped into the driveway and backed into the garage. They all followed him over.

"Hey, Evil, pretty fancy wheelie. I remember you used to do that all the time in Green Acres by your house," said Possum.

"Yeah, my bones used to bend then; now they seem to break easier, so that'll probably be the last wheelie for a while. You're not mad?" Rick asked Jules.

"No, you were wearing your helmet. Plus, there's almost no traffic on this road either. But don't do it again, Mister! Unless you can teach me how to do it too."

"We'll see. It takes time to get good at it. Maybe if we find Cindy quickly and stay here longer. I'm happy to show you for sure at some point. Thanks for not being upset with me for showing off," said Rick.

"Well, you didn't crash, and honestly, I was impressed. You looked comfortable on that bike. If you had crashed, I'd be ripping you a new one!" said Jules with a laugh.

They all went inside, and Rick showed Possum everything he had on the case so far in the war room. Malia and Jules hung out on the back deck by the water, enjoying the lightning bugs in the yard. The doorbell rang, and when Rick answered it, it was Jake. He had a big bag of aluminum trays with him.

"I hope y'all are hungry. This is the best barbecue in the area."

"Just set it on the kitchen island, and I'll set the table," said Jules.

Rick introduced everyone while Jules set the table, and they all grabbed a seat. She set all the food in the center, and they all helped themselves.

"Are you not married?" asked Rick.

"I was about five years ago. My wife was killed by a drunk driver in a head-on crash," said Jake.

"I'm so sorry," replied Rick.

"It's okay. Thank you. That event changed my perspective. I used to enjoy drinking with the guys, and I'm ashamed to admit it, but I've driven home a few times with an open beer, squinting to see the road. I sold my microbrewery soon after that. I couldn't keep making beer; it brought back too many bad memories. My daughter was studying to become a brewmaster at the time, and she continued. She was deeply affected by her mother's passing and quit drinking herself, but she still loved the craft of brewing. That's when she decided to create a line of non-alcoholic beers we could sell. She had already brought in non-alcoholic beers from other breweries to Oyster City Brewing Company where she worked, but they didn't even know she was planning to create her own brand. She wanted to market it there and give them exclusive rights for a year before we opened our own place here on St. George Island. I can show you all tomorrow. It looks like a beach house, but I had it zoned for commercial use. No one, and I mean no one, in the area had any idea that inside that beach house is a fully equipped brewery in the back, and a brewpub up front and in the backyard overlooking the bay."

"What are you going to name it?"

"Cindy came up with the name. It will be Forgotten Coast Brewing Company."

"That sounds amazing. I love the name. Jules and I stopped drinking a while back, but we still enjoy good non-alcoholic beers. I think a non-alcoholic brewpub would be very successful," said Rick.

"She's not naive either. We know we need to sell regular beer as well, but she said she wants to run it differently. Too many patrons are overserved, so she wanted to implement a breathalyzer machine at the door and offer free rides home with a small fleet of autonomous electric cars. She was working with a team at Tesla that was going to make that possible. I know it sounds crazy, but these damn cars can drive you home, drop you off, and return to base all on their own with just a little programming. No need for drivers. The breathalyzer machine would ensure that sober people weren't abusing the service," said Jake.

"That's brilliant," added Possum. "Who would program the address for the car? Would you have to pay someone to handle that?"

"No, that's the beauty of it. When someone comes in to order a beer or start a tab, they have to scan their driver's license to check if that is where they are currently staying and add an email address and phone number. When they cash out, they walk to the door and scan the back of their receipt. They then do the breathalyzer, and if they are over the limit, the machine gives them a car number. They walk to the car, get in, and it drives them home. That helps the customer and saves lives, and it also gives us an incredible amount of marketing data."

"Genius!" exclaimed Possum.

"What about their car? They have to come back and pick it up. Right?" asked Rick.

"True, they can either use Uber to go back, or we're developing a system for the cars to return to their home, where they can be scheduled to pick them up the next day at a set time.

We're also exploring an autonomous flatbed tow truck. That's a bit down the road, but Elon Musk is always pushing the limits. This low-profile truck would lift the customer's car onto a flatbed, drive them home, drop off the car, and then come back. For now, this would require a staff member here at the brewery, but I wouldn't be surprised if, when it hits the market, it comes equipped with a robot to hook up the car to the flatbed. Technology is advancing rapidly," said Jake.

"Holy shit! That's like 'The Jetsons' kind of reality," said Rick. "Or what was that movie? Uhhh, 'The Fifth Element.' Yeah, that's it."

They all sat down to enjoy the barbecue. Jules had made a big batch of sun tea earlier, and Possum had brought a Key Lime pie from Publix. After dinner, they moved to the war room to go over the case in more detail.

"Jake, how strongly do you feel that Cindy will be returned if you meet their ransom demands?" asked Rick.

"That's hard to say. I don't even know what their demands are yet."

"So, nothing since the last email?"

"Not a peep. That makes me worry," said Jake.

"Well, I have good news. We have the master hacker here now. Possum has a way with computers. I forwarded the last email you got from the kidnappers, and he is trying to find the origin. What's the status, Possum?" asked Rick.

"Luckily, the email came from a Gmail account. I tried to trace the IP address, but they were using a VPN, so that's impossible. However, I sent the email address to Carson, and he's working on getting a warrant to have Gmail reveal where the account was created. Whatever was sent went through a VPN; they probably didn't think we'd be able to do that. If they created the account on a home computer or laptop and at any point turned off the VPN or used that same device to check their email, maybe we can find a lead on the location of at least one use of that email address. I guess they only created it to send the ransom message. As soon as Carson gets back to me, I need to email them from my MacBook, which Carson will load a program into that will copy any routing or location from which the email was checked. In other words, if I email them several times at different times, maybe they will check their email on a phone or be connected to a local Wi-Fi network, and we can trace them. It's worth a shot. I will act as you, Jake, and ask what their demands are. I will pretend to be very cooperative."

"That could work," replied Jake. "Anything I can do to help?"

"Yes, as soon as I get the program installed on my MacBook, I will need your login info. I will sync our laptops with the app, that way you will see what I see. I know it sounds a bit intrusive, but we have to do whatever it takes to find these creeps."

"I have no problem with that," said Jake.

Rick thanked Jake for bringing over the food and walked him to his truck.

"Just have faith, Jake. Keeping the lines of communication open is key. They will slip up at some point."

"Thanks, Rick. I hope you're right. I need my Cindy back."

"We'll get her back."

Rick stood on the circular drive and watched as Jake drove off. He could only imagine what Jake was going through. Everyone liked Jake immediately and couldn't wait to get Cindy back and get to know her. Rick strolled back inside. They had all decided to watch a movie in the great room. The night's feature film was *Smile*. Both Rick and Jules loved horror movies, and this one scored a 6.5 on IMDb, which was quite high for that genre.

As they watched the film, Rick noticed how Possum cuddled with Malia. It was good to see Possum so happy. He had a rough bout with women after his wife was murdered, but he and Malia seemed like a perfect fit.

THREE

Rick was dreaming when the smell of bacon abruptly awoke him. He glanced at the alarm clock and saw it was 5:29 a.m. He wanted to go back to sleep, but that bacon was calling. He checked his fasting app and realized he couldn't eat for another five hours.

Possum!

Rick carefully climbed out of bed, making sure not to wake Jules. He stepped into the kitchen, expecting to see Possum, but Malia was there cooking.

"Good morning, Malia. You're up early."

"Yeah, Possum's in the war room. He had me start the bacon, and he's doing something on the phone with Carson. Want some coffee?"

Malia poured Rick a cup of black coffee, and he strolled into the war room. When he stepped inside, Possum held up one finger for Rick to wait as he talked on the phone. Rick listened and waited. Possum finally hung up.

"You're up early."

"I haven't really slept yet. I lay down after the movie and got a text from Carson. I've been up ever since. You're not gonna believe this, and I'm not sure what to make of it. Carson tapped into Jake's computer with the login info he gave him. Carson said Jake received a new email demand at 2:20 a.m. It was from the same Gmail address as before, but this time, the email originated from a device connected to Jake's router."

"What are you saying?" asked Rick.

"That the email came from a device on his property."

"What?!"

"Yep. We need to look into Jake, I'm afraid."

"Maybe he has a live-in maid or a property manager. My gut says Jake is not involved."

"Me too. There has to be another explanation. I'll head over there in a few hours. By the way, you guys are cooking bacon so early in the morning. I'm on a fasting schedule, and I should have slept a few more hours because the smell of bacon doesn't help me in my fasting endeavors. Capece?"

"I'm sorry. I wasn't thinking. There's no hiding the smell of bacon."

"Don't get me wrong. I appreciate your breakfasts and everything else you cook. I'm just a bacon nut, as you know."

"I can just cook it on the outside deck next time. Jake built a nice outdoor kitchen on the lower deck."

"That's a great compromise," said Rick.

"The funny thing is, the bacon isn't even for breakfast. I just wanted to get it cooked. Malia tried to make us seafood chef salads for lunch later."

"Oh snap! That will be amazing. I guess I'll tough it out and wait for those," said Rick.

"Look at the new email."

Possum spun his MacBook around for Rick to read.

From: CJ Cooper <CJCoop212976@gmail.com>
To: Jake Richmond <Jake_Richmond_1961@gmail.com>
Date: Fri, Nov 28, 2025, 2:07 AM
Subject: (Fair Trade)
Jake,

We have been patient with you regarding your intended new project. While you haven't broken ground yet, we have knowledge that you intend to, and that will not sit well with our ancestors. If you are willing to give up ownership of the land and mineral rights of your land Parcel ID / Account Number: 06-07S-06W-0000-0030-0100 in a blind trust to a corporation we have set up, we will release Cindy. You have one week to comply. If you do not comply, we will begin sending her to you in parts.

CJ

"I looked up that parcel in the county registrar, and it is the land right next to our beach house—approximately 132 acres," said Possum.

"But Jake already said he has no intention of developing this land. We need to have another sit-down with him. Do you think he's running some sort of insurance scam?" asked Rick.

"I honestly don't know. But we need to find out if he is the one who sent the email to himself. The email was definitely sent from his server, but there might be another explanation. We need to check if he has any surveillance footage from around the time the email was sent. We can then verify whether he was the one who sent it or if someone else from the house—or nearby with access to his router—did," said Possum.

"Okay, we should both go over there. My guess is he doesn't even know he got an email yet. If we can wake him up, we'll be able to tell. I hate to wake someone up this early, but we should go now. Since it's regarding Cindy, he'll understand. Let's roll."

Rick and Possum hopped into the Bronco and headed straight to Jake's place. When they arrived, the sun had just started to peek above the horizon. There were no lights on in the house. Rick hesitantly rang the doorbell, then pounded on the front door as if he were the police. A few moments later, Jake came to the door, wrapped in a fleece robe and squinting —clearly he had just been woken up.

"What's up, guys? Has something happened?" asked Jake.

"I'm sorry to wake you up, Jake, but it's about the email you got."

"Did you find out who sent it?"

"No, I'm referring to the new one," said Rick.

"What new one?" asked Jake.

"What time did you go to bed?" asked Rick.

"Just before midnight. Why?"

"You haven't checked your email yet?"

"No, I rarely check my email in my sleep, Rick," said Jake sarcastically. "Come on in."

Possum and Rick followed Jake into his office in his beach house.

"Let me push the coffee button. I'll be right back."

Possum and Rick sat down, and Rick motioned with his head to the surveillance camera facing Jake's laptop. Jake came back in and opened his laptop.

"Can you check it on your phone?" asked Rick as they waited for Jake's laptop to wake up.

"Nah, I'm old school. I have a flip phone."

"What about an iPad or tablet?"

"Nope, don't have one. Just my trusty Microsoft Surface, here."

Jake opened his email and read what Rick and Possum already knew was there.

"What the fuck? I have no intention of developing that parcel. We already discussed this. At one time, I was considering it, but after a meeting with the city council, I decided just to keep it as it is for my daughter and me to use. As I mentioned, we like to camp out there, ride four-wheelers, and use our metal detectors."

"When did you have that meeting with the city council?" asked Possum.

"That was about a year ago. It was right before we decided to turn that beach house into a brewery and brewpub. I was thinking about building on the land, but since we had just broken ground on several beach house rentals, I just adjusted the plans for one of them that had a big lot. I wanna show y'all today anyway. It's the place we were talking about last night," said Jake.

"Do you remember anyone being extremely vocal opposing your idea that day?" asked Rick.

"The usual suspects. There's always opposition to new developments. I actually have a copy of the meeting minutes in a file. Hang on."

Jake opened up a file cabinet and shuffled through it for a while, then pulled out a file folder.

"Here it is. Anyone who spoke is on record that day," said Jake.

"It's highly likely that the kidnapper was in that meeting. Can we get a copy of your surveillance video?" asked Possum.

"Yeah, it records to DVD. The machine is in that closet. Why?"

"Well, before I answer that, do you have anyone who works

here that would have been on your property at 2:07 a.m. last night? Or any overnight guests?"

"Uh, no. I have a maid who comes by, but she only works a couple of days a week. This house is too big for me to keep clean by myself, but she doesn't live on the property or stay over. Plus, she barely speaks English. I doubt she's our brilliant kidnapper. Why?"

"The email you got last night was sent from your router."

"No shit?!"

"No shit! Who else has your router password? You have Wi-Fi, right?"

"Yes. As far as I can remember, only Cindy and I. I had a cousin stay over, and I gave him the password, but that was about two years ago, and he lives in Chicago. He hasn't been down here since. I actually spoke to him yesterday—I called him to wish his youngest a happy birthday, and he was talking about making a trip back down but has been too busy with work. He's the only other one with the password. Lucia, my housekeeper, doesn't even use it."

Possum got up and made a copy of the last 24 hours of surveillance footage. He noted the brand of the DVR recorder and knew he could install CMS software on his MacBook that would allow him to view all the footage from every camera. They thanked Jake and made plans to meet him after lunch at the beach house he intended to use for their new brewpub.

Back in the war room, Possum downloaded Milestone XProtect Essential software to view the surveillance footage. Jake had many cameras on his property—several inside the house and numerous outside. Possum started with the camera from Jake's home office. At 4:13 p.m. that day, he closed his laptop and didn't return to the office until a few minutes before they went over to visit him. He definitely didn't send the email.

Possum went through each camera shot and focused on the time around when the email was sent. On the second-to-last one, he saw a white van pull up just before Jake's place and stop. It sat there for just a few minutes, then drove off.

"Bingo!"

That email was sent by someone in the van who had piggy-backed onto Jake's home Wi-Fi. Possum logged into Jake's router and saw an IP address connecting to his Wi-Fi at 2:05 a.m. and disconnecting at 2:08 a.m. He tried to see the license plate, but the video was too pixelated and the angle was off.

"No luck?" asked Rick.

"Besides ruling out Jake and knowing it came from inside a white Ford van, we have nothing. Can you imagine how many white Ford vans there are in the area?" asked Possum.

"Is there anything on the van or about the van that makes it stand out?" asked Rick.

Possum zoomed in and printed a photo of the van.

"I'm gonna pop the video into Final Cut Pro and use NEAT VIDEO 4 to reduce the noise. Maybe we can get a better-quality photo of it that way. It'll take about an hour."

Possum worked on the video while Rick found Jules, who was having coffee on the back deck with Choco and Chief.

"Hi, baby. Did you sleep well?"

"Yeah. I woke up, and you weren't there, but Malia told me where you and Possum went. Any luck?"

"Jake received an ominous email, and Possum tracked it to coming from Jake's Wi-Fi, but he was eliminated as the sender. It came from someone inside a white van that pulled close to his house. Possum's trying to clean up the video now so we can see if there are any distinguishing marks on the van. I might wanna borrow your keen eyes when he's done."

"No worries. I'm gonna run Malia over to Lynn's Quality

Oysters in Eastpoint to pick up some shrimp and scallops for lunch. She's making a seafood chef salad."

"Yeah, Possum told me. After lunch, we're gonna meet Jake at his new brew pub location. Wanna join us?"

"I'd love to see that. Maybe later today we can take the four-wheelers out on the empty property next to us."

"Let's plan that. I'll ride the Yamaha. Maybe Jake will join us, too."

After Jules finished her coffee, she and Malia headed to Eastpoint. Rick took Choco and Chief for a walk. He strolled over to the empty property and examined the sand for anything collectible. He found a few broken sand dollars and a dried-up horseshoe crab. He decided to grab a metal detector from the boat and returned after taking Choco and Chief home for breakfast. Possum was busy with the computer, so Rick went alone. He scanned an area near the bay for thirty minutes and found some beer cans and old nails. He then tried inland, but got no hits.

He saw a spot that had been dug before and scanned it. He got a hit and dug deep. All he found was a rusty piece of metal, but then he hit something hard, reached in, and pulled out a perfect, shiny black dovetail arrowhead. It was nearly ten inches long and flawless. He dug a little more and discovered a stash of beads. He had stumbled upon a Native American trading post. As he kept digging, he found several more artifacts. He was excited and couldn't wait to show Possum. He covered everything back up and marked the spot on his iPhone GPS. According to eBay, a similar arrowhead sold for close to $2,200. Rick jogged back to the beach house with his newfound treasures in hand.

"Possum, look what I found!"

Rick sprawled the bounty over the desk.

"Wow, where?"

"On the property next to us. I think it's an old trading post.

"That is a nice point. I bet you can get like twenty-five hundred bucks for it," said Possum.

"I found one similar on eBay for $2,220."

"But that is obsidian. It's extremely rare here."

"Why is that?" asked Rick.

"Because obsidian isn't found here; you must be right. It was probably traded here from another area by other Native Americans. Obsidian comes from out west, mostly from the Pacific Northwest. It had to have been brought here and traded for something else. Finding it here is extremely rare," said Possum.

"So, I was right. It was probably a trading post."

"All the clues point to that, especially the beads. They traded beads for all kinds of stuff. Beads were similar to currency back then," added Possum.

"I guess I need to speak to Jake. It's his property. I get the feeling, though, he'll have the mindset of finders keepers. I'll make the offer anyway. Where did Jules run off to?" asked Rick.

"Check your phone."

Rick looked down at his phone and saw a text from Jules saying she was going to drive around and try to spot the white van. She included an enhanced photo that Possum had made using his MacBook with Final Cut Pro and NEAT VIDEO 4. The circle on the photo of the plain white Ford van highlighted the driver's side rear wheel. There was an imperfection in one part of the wheel. It was very small, but once enhanced, a keen eye could see it. He immediately texted her back.

If you find the van, do not engage.

He didn't get a reply and knew telling Jules what to do was usually a waste of time. He had to try, though.

"How did you spot the imperfection in the van's wheel, Possum?"

"I didn't. Jules did. She and Malia are driving around in the Bronco looking for it. Apalachicola isn't a big town, and it's probably a waste of time, but they might get lucky."

"I just texted her and told her not to engage. Great job on that enhanced photo, by the way. Can I see the before again?" asked Rick.

Possum pulled up both photos and placed them side by side on his MacBook. The original was too pixelated to spot the imperfection, but once enhanced, Rick was able to see it because he knew where to look.

"Damn, she has a good eye. I would've never seen it myself," said Rick.

"Yeah, I looked at it for a long time. I was focused on the paint and possible dings, but she spotted it right away. Don't worry; they are both packing. I told Jules the same thing you texted her. I doubt she'll listen, but at least they have protection."

"Let's hope for once she does listen," said Rick.

Rick took his new treasures to the garage and set up a folding table to clean them. He decided to call Jake and ask him to come over to see the bounty and update him. He picked up on the third ring.

"Hey, Rick. What's up?"

"Do you have a few minutes to swing by? I wanna show you something. I'm in the garage."

"Sure. I'll be right over."

Rick continued cleaning and sorting the native relics he discovered, and within ten minutes, Jake pulled up.

"Hey, Rick. Whatcha got there?"

"I found these while metal detecting over by the bay on your property. Check this one out."

Rick handed Jake the obsidian point.

"Damn. Shiny, ain't it? I ain't ever seen one like that before."

"They are rare. It's obsidian. They don't have those kinds of stones around here. They are mostly found around the Pacific Northwest and in Yellowstone."

"Why the hell was it here then?" asked Jake.

"It was brought here and traded, like these beads. I think I stumbled upon an old Native American trading post. Since I found it on your property, it all belongs to you."

"Nonsense. You found it. Possession is nine-tenths of the law."

"Thanks, Jake. I'm glad to hear that. You don't seem surprised that I found all this stuff."

"Because I'm not. My daughter and I have found all kinds of Native American stuff out there. Not the obsidian before, which is cool, but other things," said Jake.

"Do you think the kidnapper is referring to what's under the sand in his emails when he mentioned ancestors?"

"I was wondering about that. It could be someone who has relatives buried there. I've never found any human remains, though. Or it could just be a diversion to throw us off."

"For sure. Both are possibilities. Is there anything about the property that stands out to you or that you haven't told me yet?" asked Rick.

"No, not really. Well, oh yeah, I did have a man come by here a few months ago. He was a *Land Man*, like the TV show of the same name. He wanted to do some testing to see if there was any oil or natural gas. They came out and did whatever it is they do and reported back to me that it was dry here and there was no chance of oil or mineral wealth. I completely forgot about that because it came up dry and slipped my mind."

"Land man, huh? Do you have a copy of that report?" asked Rick.

"Yeah, it's in my office somewhere. I can scan it and email it to you."

"Sounds good."

"Listen, we are trying to locate that white van that piggy-backed onto your Wi-Fi. It's a needle in a haystack but you never know. We might get lucky."

"Alright, Rick. Keep up the good work. I'll stop by my home office and email you those files."

Jake drove off, and Rick continued to clean the artifacts he had found. It was quite a motherlode.

CHAPTER

FOUR

J ules drove slowly down Sawyer Lane, then turned left onto St. Vincent's Street. Spotting a white van—a late-year model Ford—she needed to get a closer look at the driver's side rear wheel. The van pulled into the Apalachicola Dog Park and parked. A young guy in shorts and a golf shirt stepped out with a long-haired poodle mix and opened the gate to the park. Jules parked on St. Vincent Street and double-backed, keeping the van and the young man between her. She walked up to the van and leaned over to inspect the wheels.

Wrong van.

She high-tailed it back to the Bronco. It was the third possible van they had already checked out. She was surprised at how many white Ford vans she noticed. She knew they were always around. But it's like when someone tells you to watch out for a yellow Jeep. You'll suddenly notice lots of yellow Jeeps. Your mind doesn't focus on random things like that unless you tell it to.

Malia was marking off the license plates and addresses of the white vans they had spotted, hoping to avoid wasting time on duplicates. Jules texted Rick, telling him they'd be back soon for Malia to make the seafood chef salad.

No hurry. Any luck?

Lots of white vans. All the wrong ones so far.

Jules turned onto Avenue L and, at the corner of Avenue L and 12th Street, spotted a van parked under a carport beside a dilapidated duplex. She walked around the side of the house, peeking into the carport, and noticed a flaw on the driver's side rear wheel. The photo on her phone matched exactly. Despite Rick's objections, she decided to use a tactic and knock on the door.

A young guy, smelling of weed, answered.

"Can I help you?" he asked.

"Hi, my name is Valentina. We are offering a Google Earth program in your area and wondered if you had a minute to discuss it. Is that your van?"

"Nah, my roommate's. Hang on, I'll get him."

A moment passed, and Jules overheard the roommate telling him to ask her to leave. The original guy returned to the door.

"He's not interested."

"Oh, that's too bad because it's a government program that actually pays owners of vehicles to mount a camera on their cars or trucks to automatically photograph the area to help with details on the Google Earth page."

"How much does it pay?"

"Depends on how much you drive around, but most people earn five hundred to seven hundred dollars a month. It's a 90-day program," said Jules.

"Cory!" yelled the man. "Come here, man. You gotta hear this."

Moments later, an equally stoned dude in a ripped T-shirt and flip-flops joined them. The roommate explained what Jules had just said.

"I just want to ask a few more questions, and then we can get you signed up," she said.

"Okay, shoot," said the stoner.

"What year is your van?"

"It's a 2003 Ford Econoline E-150," he replied.

"How often do you drive it in the area?"

"Pretty much daily. Depends on what's going on with work."

"What do you do for work?" asked Jules.

"I'm a freelance IT guy."

"Oh, okay, so computers and stuff?"

"Sort of. Mostly online tech stuff like managing networks, developing software, analyzing data, and protecting against cyber-attacks."

"Interesting."

"It's a job," he shrugged.

"Do you ever drive over to St. George Island?"

"Sometimes, not too often."

"When was the last time you drove over there?" asked Jules.

"What does it matter?"

"It's just so we can develop a baseline area for you in the Google Earth maps."

Jules noted that the last question made him nervous. She sensed she was onto something and decided to push the envelope. Neither guy was particularly big, and she had her handgun in the small of her back. Looking straight at him, she asked,

"Did you drive over there last night and stop in front of 601 E. Pine Ave?"

The guy looked stunned, his mouth dropping open in shock.

"What is this? Are you a cop?"

"No, I'm a private detective. I know you stopped in front of Jake Richmond's house and sent an email to him through his router and Wi-Fi."

Sweat began to bead on the guy's forehead, and he started to shake. Jules reached behind her back and wrapped her fingers around the handle of her pistol. Suddenly, he stood up and moved toward her. She whipped out her semi-automatic pistol and aimed it at his chest.

"Sit down now! Or I'll put a hole in you!"

He plopped down on the couch, visibly trembling.

"Where is she?"

"Where is who?"

"Cindy Richmond. I know you kidnapped her."

"Lady, are you crazy? I haven't kidnapped anyone! A guy at Bar 98 gave me $300 to hack into that Wi-Fi router and send a prewritten email. I didn't even read it. He told me not to."

"What guy?"

"I don't know. Some guy sat down beside me there one day. I overheard someone call him Swift Eagle. That's all I know. I swear!"

"Can you describe him?"

"He was tall, dark, had long black hair, and wore a beaded headband. I think he's native."

"Okay, don't tell anyone I came by. I will send a sketch artist by soon. Do as he says. If you tell anyone, especially that Swift Eagle guy, I will return in the middle of the night and put two in you. One in the head and one in the chest. Your room-mate too."

"What kind of PI are you?!" he asked, fear in his eyes.

"I lied. I'm not a detective. I work for one of the alphabet agencies. Capece?"

"CIA?"

"Something like that. You're on a need-to-know basis. And right now, you don't need to know."

Jules stood up and walked backward out the door with her weapon drawn. She was both excited to tell Rick and scared to share the news. She knew he would be upset with her for going in alone; it was reckless. Still, she had broken the first clue in the case.

As they drove back, Jules felt the guy had been honest with her. He didn't seem like the mastermind behind a kidnapping with ransom demands. She decided to call Carson before returning to the beach house.

"Jules?"

"Hi, Carson. I know Rick usually calls you, but I need some help. We're in a small town in the Panhandle, Apalachicola, and the cops here are virtually non-existent. Can you help me find a sketch artist? I need one yesterday."

"Let me call you back in a few minutes."

Jules pulled over just before the bridge to St. George Island and waited. She figured if she brought Rick two pieces of good news, he'd be more understanding of her risky choice. As she sat and waited, her irritation with herself increased. She should have waited for Rick or someone for backup; going into that house alone was unacceptable. Ever since being carjacked a few years back, she had developed a strong will to take care of things herself. But today's decision had been downright reckless. She promised herself she'd contact her therapist once back to figure out why she had made such a dangerous choice.

After about fifteen minutes, Carson called back.

"Jules, I have a guy in Tallahassee who works for the FLDE. He's en route now. I gave him your number—expect a call shortly. He'll need the address."

"Wow, thanks, Carson. That was fast!"

"Yeah, caught him at the right time. If you need anything else, just give me a call or text," said Carson.

"I appreciate it. I'll keep you posted."

Jules ended the call and crossed the bridge. As she approached the beach house, her anxiety grew. She pulled into the circular drive and saw Rick in the garage. She asked Malia to let her tell Rick alone, and she walked into the house to find Possum.

"Hi, baby. Any luck?"

"You could say that. We found the van."

Before she could continue, Rick blurted out, "No shit? That's great! Okay, I'll call the local police, see if they can secure a warrant, and put together a SWAT team to take him down."

Rick grabbed his phone.

"Rick, wait, wait. You don't need to call."

"What?" asked Rick, looking perplexed.

"I already interviewed the guy."

"You what? I told you not to contact him. He could be a murderer. He's already a kidnapper. What were you thinking?"

"I know. I know. It was stupid, and I'm sorry. I guess I got so excited, I jumped the gun."

Jules recounted how she came up with the whole Google Earth scheme on the spot, entered the house, and scared the guy straight. She also mentioned the sketch artist coming down from Tallahassee. When she finished, she braced for Rick's explosion. Instead, he grinned and hugged her tightly.

"I don't know what I would've done if something bad happened to you."

Tears rolled down Jules' cheeks. She knew she had acted impulsively, even if it had led to a breakthrough in the case. She told Rick she would call her therapist. She was happier than ever, loved Rick, and didn't have a death wish. She needed to understand why she put herself in such danger.

"You're not mad?"

"No. Let's call it even since you didn't get mad at me for riding wheelies on the street the other day."

"I love you, Rick Waters. We're even."

Rick showed Jules all the native artifacts he had discovered, and they planned to go back out after lunch.

After Rick finished cleaning up, he joined the gang in the dining room for lunch. Malia had made the seafood chef salad she promised and even rolled her own sushi with fresh tuna she had picked up at the market.

"Holy crap, Malia. This is incredible! How did you learn to roll your own sushi?"

"It's not hard. Growing up in Hawaii, it was common to roll sushi. I have a little kit with a bamboo roller and other items. The trick is the rice—you have to use good sticky rice," Malia explained.

"Well, you nailed it. Are these spicy tuna rolls?"

"Yep. Try the dipping sauce too. They are great with soy or the dipping sauce."

"Damn! You're right. What is that?"

"Family secret. It doesn't matter, I'll tell you. It's mayo with sriracha, a little soy sauce, and honey. I also added a bit of cayenne to liven it up."

"It's a winner! You need to hang onto her, Possum. She's a keeper."

"I intend to, Rick," said Possum, mouth full.

After lunch, they decided to pick out off-road toys and scout out Jake's property. As Rick was getting on the Yamaha YZ 125, his phone rang. He ripped off his helmet.

"Hey, y'all, it's Gary."

"Hey, Gary! Where in the world are you?"

"I'm in Tallahassee. We took delivery of the new 737 jet, and Clay finished his training. We did a little test flight and thought we'd come hang with y'all for a few days. Clay is gonna fly the jet back to Dallas for a few upgrades, but I rented a car. I'm driving your way now. Do you have room at the beach house for us?"

"Aw, hell yeah! Y'all come on down. I'll send you the address. We're about to head out on the property with some four-wheelers and a motorcycle. When you get here, I'll text you, and you and Kelly can grab one and meet us. It's the perfect place to ride. I'm glad y'all are coming! I need Kelly's help reading the seismic report Jake got on the property from a landman. It's an oil-and-gas survey or something. I can't make heads or tails of it."

"Okay, I'll drive faster. We're about half an hour away now in the rental car."

"Alright, Gary. Drive fast, take chances. See you soon."

Rick put his cell phone in his front pocket and strapped on his helmet.

"Let's go exploring!" he exclaimed.

Jules chose a four-wheeler, while Possum and Malia hopped into a Can-Am side-by-side. There were still plenty of toys left in the garage. Rick texted Gary the address and the garage code, and they headed across the sand.

They found a trail Jake had made over the years, filled with berms and whoops. Rick was in his element, catching air and tearing through the sand like he used to when he raced motocross. It felt great to be back in the saddle. Jules kept pace with him but had to slow down occasionally for Possum and Malia to catch up. Rick couldn't remember the last time he'd had so much fun. He promised himself he'd buy a new dirt bike when he got home and ride more. Jules was enjoying herself too.

When they stopped at the end of the property bordering the state park, they took off their helmets and burst into laughter. It was infectious. Since motorized off-road vehicles aren't allowed in St. George Island State Park, that was the end of that trail. Rick really wanted to see the end of the island and suggested they return another day by bicycle. They decided to explore off the trail and around to the bay side. It was a bit slower but incredibly scenic. They reached a spot where the sand met the bay—firm and fast, like a racetrack. Rick gave Jules a look, and they both took off like bats out of hell.

They arrived at a clearing where Jake had mentioned he liked to camp with his daughter. It had a large fire ring and stacks of firewood. They decided to take a break and build a fire. Just then, Rick's phone whistled—Gary was announcing his arrival. Rick sent the location via Google pin and stoked the fire.

Within about fifteen minutes, he could hear the unmistakable sound of an approaching side-by-side.

"Hey, Gary!" yelled Rick.

Rick walked over and hugged Kelly as Gary ripped the big cooler off the back of his side-by-side.

"Of course, you brought a cooler," said Rick.

"I'm always prepared like a Boy Scout."

"Maybe a drunk Boy Scout."

"Ha-fucking-ha. I guess you don't want a Collective Arts Hazy IPA then? I'll just leave them in the cooler."

That was Rick's favorite non-alcoholic beer. He looked at Gary with puppy dog eyes, begging for forgiveness for the drunk Boy Scout comment. Gary laughed and tossed Rick a Collective Arts beer. They all sat around the fire on large wooden logs Jake had placed there years before. There was even an outhouse at the campsite.

They listened to the latest adventure Gary and Kelly had been on. Gary and Rick had gone to high school together and reconnected a few years later. Gary had bought a Powerball ticket at a gas station one day after work with the change he got from filling up and a few beers. He ended up winning one of the largest Powerball jackpots in U.S. history. Wisely, he invested some of it and continued to grow his future, eventually joining Rick as a partner in his private detective and boat charter business.

Kelly was working as a bartender, waiting to land a position as a geologist in a mine in the Congo when Gary met her. After he purchased the mine, he put Kelly in charge of both the mineral and diamond mines. They eloped and have been together ever since.

"Rick, I got a sketch from the artist. Look," said Jules, passing her phone to Rick.

The sketch depicted a man resembling a Native American from a movie set. He wore a beaded headband, had a long, straight nose, high cheekbones, and long straight black hair parted in the middle, with no facial hair. He reminded Rick of a sketch he'd seen of Sitting Bull years ago.

"That may be our kidnapper," said Rick.

They all sat around the fire, drinking, laughing, and sharing stories until late afternoon.

"Y'all wanna head back? I want to show Kelly some geological surveys when we get back to the beach house," Rick suggested.

"I'm happy to look at them, Rick," said Kelly.

Rick fired up his Yamaha YZ 125 and threw sand over the fire. Possum finished it off and made sure it was completely out. Then he and Malia hopped into the side-by-side and followed Gary, Kelly, and Jules back to the beach house.

Once they got back, Rick pulled out the hose and washed all the toys. Gary helped him put everything away in the garage. Possum and Malia drove into town in the Bronco and returned with supplies for a BBQ. He planned to make burgers, chicken sandwiches, and hot dogs—simple but all-American barbecue. Possum loved to cook and was a master at grilling. He picked up a brisket but planned to smoke it all night for the next day.

Gary plopped down in a deck chair and cracked open a Busch Light tallboy. Money hadn't changed him; he was still as down-to-earth as ever. He could buy half the town and still have money left in the bank, but he never carried himself that way. Kelly joined Rick in the war room to review the geology files Jake had sent him.

CHAPTER
FIVE

T he barbecue had been perfect. Rick had eaten too many hot dogs and was feeling bloated. Kelly, still poring over the files Jake had sent, called him over.

"Rick, this report does indeed show there is little to no evidence that there are any rare earth minerals, oil, or natural gas under this property. So the oil man was right when he told Jake that."

"I see," replied Rick.

"There's just one problem," Kelly added.

"What's that?"

"This file is not for this property. You see the codes here?" asked Kelly.

Rick leaned in closer, examining the codes she indicated.

"This BASA, which is short for basil salt. And this is RDCH, which is high-density red clay. Those types of earth aren't found around here, and you know what is missing?"

"What?" Rick asked, curious.

"250510!"

"Oh, well, that clears it up," Rick said sarcastically. "Okay, what is 250510?"

"That's the code for silica sands and quartz sands—only the most prominent type of soil on the property."

"So it's fake?"

"No, it's not a fake. What's fake is that this geological test was not done here. It was done somewhere else, maybe Oklahoma. It fits the type of earth in that area."

"So the oilman lied to Jake? Why?"

"Consider it. If there is oil, natural gas, or rare earth minerals beneath his property, wouldn't it be more costly to buy from him? Or maybe even ransom from him!"

"So that creates motive. We need to find out who this guy is. The name signed on this is not someone listed on the National Geographic survey database. So, it's probably not his real name. He could be the key to finding Cindy," Kelly said.

"What's the next move?"

"I need to rent a portable seismic monitor and run some tests. We'll need permission from Jake to make some... explosions."

"Explosions?"

"Yes. I need to run some control blasts, and I can rent a Geodevice Sigma-4 in Tallahassee. Gary and I can go there in the morning. If you can get written permission from Jake, we can test sometime after lunch. I'll get a Geiger counter too for the REEs."

"REEs?" Rick asked.

"Sorry, I'm in full geologist mode. Rare earth elements. The media usually calls them rare earth minerals. The actual name is REE."

"Got it. I'll talk to Jake in the morning."

Rick and Kelly joined the rest of the gang on the upper rear deck. It was a perfect night, and they enjoyed laughter and conversation until the early hours. Rick and Jules finally slipped into bed around 1:20 a.m.

~

When Rick zombie-walked into the kitchen for coffee, Possum informed him that Gary and Kelly had left around 6:00 a.m. for Tallahassee.

"I'll holler at Jake after I finish my coffee. I'm looking forward to blowing up some stuff!"

"Rick, you realize those are controlled blasts in holes we have to dig, right?"

"Oh, no, I didn't know that."

"By the way, Gary took the Bronco instead of the rental, saying he needed to tow something back."

"All good."

Rick finished his coffee and called Jake.

"Hi, Jake. I have some updates for you. Can you swing by?"

"Sure, I'll be right over."

Rick poured himself another cup of coffee, inhaling the rich aroma of the brisket Possum had been smoking overnight; it made his mouth water. Just then, a knock interrupted him. Jake peeked his head inside.

"Rick, you here?"

"Yep, come on in."

"Can you take a ride with me? I have to run by the court-house real quick. You can update me en route."

"Sure, no problem. I'll be right there. Let me tell Jules."

Rick jogged outside and climbed into Jake's Range Rover.

"Nice ride," Rick commented.

"Thanks. I'm really a Ford guy, but I bought this at an

auction to resell it. I flip cars for fun, honestly. But after driving this, I realized I couldn't let it go; I fell in love with it."

"I can see why. It rides like a dream."

On the drive, Rick showed Jake the artist's rendering of the possible kidnapper and updated him on the geological reports. He had gotten permission to conduct additional testing, even notarizing the document Kelly had prepared the night before.

On the ride back from the courthouse, a big red pickup truck suddenly loomed in Jake's rearview mirror. Assuming the driver would pass on the bridge, Jake slowed down. But instead, the man in the truck slammed into them, almost knocking Jake off the road.

"What the fuck?!"

Suddenly, the rear glass shattered as someone in the truck fired a gun at them. Instinctively, Rick reached for his handgun and realized he hadn't brought it. The truck bumped the Range Rover several more times, and Jake sped up, trying to lose him. The truck hit the Range Rover at an angle as they approached the bottom of the bridge, causing the Range Rover to spin uncontrollably and then start rolling. It flipped several times and came to rest upside down at the water's edge.

Rick was stunned and had lost consciousness for a minute. When he got his bearings back, he worked feverishly to loosen the seat belt holding him upside down. Blood was dripping down Jake's forehead, pooling on the headliner

"Jake, are you okay? Jake!" yelled Rick, panic rising in his throat.

Jake didn't respond. A faint smell of smoke began to fill the vehicle, and Rick, still hanging upside down, struggled to release the seat belt. With his Leatherman in his pocket, he fished it out with shaky hands, grasping a ceiling beam to avoid slamming his head as he cut himself free.

He lowered himself out, opening the passenger door, but the wreckage had smashed it shut. Smoke billowed now from the hood, enveloping the SUV. Rick climbed back in through the passenger side and sliced through Jake's seat belt. Jake's body slumped over the wheel, unconscious.

and onto the ceiling. Rick grabbed his arms and pulled with all his might. He finally made some progress and dragged Jake out to the sand. The smoke was getting thicker and darker, so he dragged Jake a bit farther away from the SUV and placed his head on the grass.

"Shit, my phone!"

Rick ran back to the SUV and stuck his head inside. He spotted his phone lying by the sun visor on the front windshield. He grabbed it and ran back to Jake as he called 911. He wasn't worried about the SUV exploding, per se, but it was going to burn to the ground soon. Most cars only blew up in movies.

"911, what is your emergency?"

"I need an ambulance, fire truck, and police to the south side of St. George Island Bridge. We were shot at and forced off the road. My friend's SUV is on fire."

"Is anyone hurt?"

"Yes, my friend has a bad cut on his upper forehead. He's breathing but unresponsive. He has a good pulse."

"Okay, sir, help is on the way. What is your name?"

"I'm Rick Waters, and my injured friend is Jake Richmond."

"Okay, Mr. Waters. Stay on the line. They should be arriving shortly."

Rick ripped part of his shirt off, wrapping it around Jake's head to slow the bleeding. The air thick with smoke, he squinted, barely able to see the Range Rover as it became engulfed. He remembered Jake had put his briefcase in the back seat, likely very important. Knowing the risk, he dashed over, flinging open the rear passenger door as it fell out, leaning against the door.

Rick grabbed the briefcase and ran back, the metal hot against his hands. He tossed it onto the sand and glanced at his palms, realizing he had burned some skin.

When the ambulance and fire truck finally arrived, EMTs quickly assessed Jake's vitals before placing him inside the ambulance, still unconscious. A second ambulance attended to Rick's burnt hands. The firefighters extinguished the flames swiftly, but it was evident that the Range Rover was a total loss.

Once the police showed up, Rick provided a statement, detailing the encounter and the red Dodge truck. They offered him a ride to the hospital, and though he felt a flicker of anxiousness—his previous experience in a cop car had been handcuffed and apprehensive—he accepted the offer.

As they pulled into George E. Weems Memorial Hospital, the officer handed Rick his business card.

"Take care," he said.

"Thanks," Rick replied, heading to the receptionist.

"Hi, I'm looking for an update on Jake Richmond."

"Are you family?"

"Yes, ma'am. I'm his stepbrother."

Rick knew how hospitals worked and crossed his fingers, hoping that the lie would hold up.

"He's in stable condition, in the ICU and still unconscious. Have a seat; I'll let you know when he's in a room for visitors."

Rick walked back to the waiting area, setting Jake's brief-case down. There was little he could do for now, so he called Gary.

"Hey, Gary, where are the keys for your rental? I need a lift. I'm at the George E. Weems Memorial Hospital."

"Oh shit. Are you hurt?"

"No, not really. Just a few burns on my palms. Long story. I need Jules or Possum to come pick me up; Possum said you had to borrow the Bronco."

"Listen, I'm almost in Apalachicola. I can swing by and pick you up. It'll be faster."

Fifteen minutes later, Gary walked in, accompanied by Kelly. Rick checked on Jake once more, but there was still no update, so he walked over to Gary and Kelly.

"What happened?" Gary asked as he put the Bronco in drive.

"Someone in a red Dodge truck tried to run us off the road and kill us. They shot at us and did some kind of PIT maneuver, causing us to flip several times. Jake's Range Rover caught fire. That's when I burnt my hands trying to get this damn briefcase out. Stupid!" said Rick, frustration seeping through.

As they crested the bridge, Rick saw a tow truck flipping the Range Rover onto a flatbed.

"That was us!" he exclaimed, pointing at the burned-out SUV.

"Damn, that thing is scorched."

"Like my hands. Guess I'll be wearing gloves for a while."

"I'm glad you're alright. What's the deal with Jake?"

"I don't know. I hope it's just a concussion and not something serious. Time will tell."

Gary pulled into the circular drive and parked. They all walked inside, and as soon as Jules saw Rick with his cut shirt and bandaged hands, her jaw dropped.

"What happened?" she asked, rushing to him.

"I'm okay. Let's sit down on the deck, and I'll tell you what happened."

Everyone followed Rick outside, where he retold his

harrowing tale for the third time. The overwhelming aroma of brisket wafted through the air, replacing the smell of burnt rubber that had lingered in his nostrils.

"What time is lunch?" Rick asked.

"Well, I was thinking we should have the brisket for dinner; it needs to rest a little. I can whip up some burgers or chicken sandwiches if you want," Possum offered.

"I could go for a burger. No hot dogs, please! I stuffed myself with three of those damn things yesterday."

"I gotcha, hombre. Medium?"

"Yeah, thanks."

Jules brought Rick a tall glass of freshly brewed sun tea, which hit the spot perfectly. After lunch, Rick showed Gary a makeshift trail he could follow in the Bronco to test the land for oil, natural gas, or rare earth elements. He shared the route from his iPhone to Gary's, and soon Gary and Kelly headed off in the Bronco with the auger in tow. Gary promised Rick he'd text him once the holes were dug and the explosives set. Despite the burns on his hands, Rick was determined not to miss the upcoming boom.

Rick fell asleep in a lounge chair, and Jules had to wake him when Gary texted.

"Rick, we're all gonna go. I'll drive the Can-Am; you're in no shape to ride the dirt bike," said Jules.

Rick knew she was right but felt disappointed at missing out. His palms were too tender for now, but he thought he might be able to ride in a few days with thick gloves. He climbed into the passenger seat, and Jules followed the map on Rick's phone to the testing site. When they arrived, Kelly had headphones on and was adjusting the equipment, while Gary was casually sipping a Busch Light.

Possum and Malia arrived shortly after.

"Y'all ready to blow some shit up?" Rick called.

Gary laughed, and Kelly just shook her head, smirking. She pulled off her headphones, made a few last-minute adjustments, then replaced them.

"You wanna do the honors, Rick?"

"Hell yeah!"

Rick followed Kelly about fifty yards from the blast site. They all gathered around, and she handed him a box with four toggle switches.

"Does four toggles mean four explosions?" Rick asked, excitement bubbling up.

"That's right. Four toggles, four booms," Kelly confirmed.

Rick's eyes sparkled like a kid in a candy store.

"Okay, everybody, stay still. Here goes the first one."

He slowly reached for the top switch and pushed it up. A muffled sound echoed from the designated blast area.

"That's it?" Rick asked, disappointment creeping in.

"Yep, that's it. Three more to go," Kelly replied.

Frustration flashed across his face as he activated each toggle one by one at Kelly's signal, with each explosion proving underwhelming. Just as he reached for the last switch, Gary interrupted.

"Rick, this one is for you."

"Well, four is Jules' favorite number," Rick joked.

He flipped the toggle, and a massive explosion erupted, hurling sand and debris fifty feet into the air. The ground shook beneath them, and everyone froze, stunned.

"Kaboom!"

"Holy shit! That was huge!" Rick exclaimed.

"It wasn't part of the test. Kelly only needed three. I bought three sticks of dynamite and thought you'd like that one. I only buried it a few inches under the sand," Gary said, grinning.

"Thanks, Gary. That was cool as hell!"

"Is Hell cool? I thought it was hot. That's an oxymoron, like fast as fuck or hot as shit," Gary teased.

"You know what I meant, smartass! Anyway, thanks for that; it made my day."

"Kelly, I got a weird reading from that last explosion. Can you set it again near the same spot?"

"Hell yeah!" Rick said, excitement reigniting.

Gary reset three sticks of dynamite in the same area. Once he gave Rick the thumbs up, Rick looked to Kelly, who put on her headphones and gave him the nod. He flipped the toggle again.

"Kaboom!"

Once more, sand flew fifty feet into the air. Kelly shook her head in disbelief.

"If this reading is correct, this property sits on a massive oil and natural gas reserve. I need to connect this to my laptop and check a few things. Also, the area below the surface is packed with monazite. It's extremely rare in Florida and almost never found here. It's essential for EV batteries and magnets."

Falls back onto the ground, as if struck by lightning, she threw her arms in the air, shouting,

"Woohoo! This is my first huge find!"

They all walked back to the blast site, and Rick helped Gary put away all the gear.

This was fun, but I'm starting to think the person who submitted the faux mineral report to Jake is involved in Cindy's kidnapping. There's definitely a motive there. I mean, if Jake thought the land had no mineral value, he'd probably give it up to save Cindy more easily. I'm sure he'd give it up even if it were valuable, but I wonder if there was ever an attempt to buy it. I need to talk to Jake," said Rick.

"All I know is, the longer Cindy is captive, the less chance we have of getting her back alive. Statistically speaking," Gary added grimly.

"I know. That fact hasn't left my mind. That TV show, *The First 48*, keeps popping into my head."

Rick's phone pinged, and a big smile spread across his face.

"The nurse just texted me that Jake is conscious and has been moved to a regular room. I gave her my number and asked her to keep me posted. She thinks I'm related to Jake. You know how hospitals work."

"Oh yeah, why don't you and Jules head back? We can take care of the rest of this," Gary suggested.

Possum approached with a mischievous grin on his face.

"I have an idea. What if Jake puts the land up for auction, saying he wants to sell it because he has no plans to develop it and needs the money for his new brewpub? Gary could be the highest bidder. Don't worry, Jake's not really selling it; we can ask for closed bids to find out who the bidders are. The highest bidder will know the value of the mineral rights. Everyone else won't."

"You freaking genius. I love it. Jake will need to keep the land's value under wraps."

Rick and Jules departed in a side-by-side and headed back to the beach house. They quickly changed and hopped in the Bronco. On the way to the hospital, Rick laid out the entire auction plan to Jules.

When they arrived, the receptionist informed them that Jake was in room 222, and they made their way there.

"Well, look who's awake!" Rick said, smiling broadly as he stepped into the room.

Jake grinned back.

"Worst non-hangover ever."

"What did the doc say?" asked Rick, stepping closer.

"I have a concussion. I'll be a bit foggy for a few days, but no permanent brain damage, thank God!"

"That's such great news, Jake!"

"What do you remember about the crash?"

"The last thing I recall is losing control of the Range Rover. Can you fill me in?"

"Sorry to say, but the Range Rover is toast. Literally. It burned to the ground."

"Oh shit. Is that how you hurt your hands? I noticed the bandages and was about to ask."

"Sort of. I cut myself loose, then cut your seatbelt and dragged you out while it was just smoking. I ran back to grab your briefcase from the back seat; it was so hot that it burned my palms. No big deal."

"You dragged me out?"

"Yeah, of course. You were out cold."

"Rick, you saved my life."

"You would've done the same thing, Jake."

"I won't forget it. Trust me. But you should've left that briefcase. My accountant, Ron, has duplicates of all my files. We could've gotten the blasting release notarized again. What's happening with that now?"

"That's part of why we came by. Hang on."

Rick closed the door, lowering his voice as he explained.

"Listen, you're not gonna believe this, but that land you own, which has the worthless mineral rights report, is sitting on a gold mine. Black gold. A huge store of REEs, oil, and natural gas. It's worth billions."

"Are you serious?"

"Dead serious. Possum came up with a plan. He wants you to announce a public auction of the land to the highest bidder.

We'll ensure Gary is the highest bidder to flush out possible interest, but I suspect the second-highest bidder will be much higher than everyone else, indicating they know the land has value. Don't worry; Gary won't take possession. It's a ruse to draw out the kidnapper."

"That's a great idea."

"The key is to not let anyone know how valuable the mineral rights are. We can't tell anyone. I mean, anyone. Not even people you trust. Understand?"

"I got it. Listen, write down this number. It's for my accountant. His name is Gabe. He can get you anything you need to get the land auction set up."

"Okay, thanks, Jake. We will keep him in the dark too. No one can know. No one!"

"I understand. Gabe's a good guy. Took over for my last accountant two years ago. But he doesn't need to know about the oil find. The doctor wants to keep me here a couple of days, but between my accountant and lawyer, you'll have everything you need."

"Alright, Jake. Just get well, and we'll handle everything else. We're gonna find the son of a bitch that took Cindy and nail him to the wall."

CHAPTER
SIX

The office was nondescript—just an old converted house near downtown Apalachicola. Rick opened the door, and a secretary greeted him.

"Hi, I have an eleven o'clock with Gabe. I'm a little early."

"All good. Make yourself a coffee or latte if you wish. Gabe is just finishing up with another client. He'll be out shortly," said the woman as she pointed at the Nespresso machine.

Rick wandered over, examining the various flavors. He remembered enjoying one of those machines before and chose a Holiday Blend. After brewing a double shot, he settled into a chair. A few minutes later, Gabe stepped out, escorting a client who nodded and walked out the door.

"Mr. Waters?"

"Yeah, call me Rick."

Rick followed Gabe into his office and sat down. Gabe pushed a coaster over to Rick so he could put his latte down on his desk.

"Alright, Jake filled me in that you are assisting him with a land auction."

"Yes," Rick confirmed.

"How do you know Jake?" Gabe asked.

"I'm working with him to help find his daughter."

"That's tragic. We all pray she's returned safely. I'm a little confused, though. You're assisting Jake with a land auction? Are you a tracker or...?"

"I'm a private detective."

"That just confuses me more. Why is Jake having a private detective assist him in a land auction? No offense, but are you an auctioneer or a broker?"

"No. Jake trusts me. The ransom note forbade him from developing the land. We believe the kidnappers are local and want the land to be left untouched, so he will sell it and include a clause that it remains undeveloped and cannot be built on," said Rick.

"I understand. What about the mineral rights?"

"It's worthless. Anyone who buys it would be wasting their money. There's no value in the mineral rights. He had a test done a while back, and it came back with no oil, natural gas, or REEs. It's just sand. Nothing more."

"I see, so there won't be a clause that the land can't be drilled on?"

"Exactly. There's no need. It's worthless. We believe whoever took Cindy is either an indigenous person or some kind of crazy activist who wants to keep the land untouched. Since Jake hasn't developed it, but rumors went out that he was considering it, that caused them to jump into action. It's not like he had it for sale or anything," said Rick.

"True, it's not like he hasn't received many offers to buy it over the years. He always turned them down. That's partially why I was surprised that he wanted to auction it off now."

"I think he just wants to get Cindy back," Rick replied. "Whoever took her won't release her until they are sure the land will stay undeveloped. And as long as Jake owns it, there's always a chance he could change his mind. If it's rezoned in the auction as protected land, they will let her go. He doesn't need the land and only uses it for camping and off-roading anyway."

"Okay, I have everything I need. I can follow up with you and Jake. I'll get the rezoning handled with a local broker who works with the city. We should be able to prepare for auction in a couple of days."

"Perfect. Nice to meet you, Gabe. Have a great day."

"You too, Rick. I'm sure I'll speak to you again soon."

Rick drove back to the beach house, where he found Possum on the deck, peering through binoculars at the water.

"What's up, buddy?" Rick asked.

"You see that boat way over there?"

"Yep."

"Well, it passed by here a half-dozen times, slowing down each time it got close to the beach house. I hid behind the drapes inside and peeked out. Whoever is on it has been looking at the house through binoculars."

"Really? Maybe we should pay them a quick visit. Grab your shotgun from the motorhome, and I'll bring my pistol. Where's everyone?"

"Gary took the girls out on four-wheelers."

"At least someone is enjoying themselves. Now it's our turn."

Rick met Possum on the big catamaran and fired it up. As soon as Possum released the lines from the dock, Rick pushed the throttle forward, heading straight toward the boat that had been spying. When they got close, the boat shot out of the water and sped down the bay toward open sea. Rick couldn't catch it, but he did manage to get the name off the stern: *Jersey Boyz*.

It looked like an Axopar Aft Cabin with four massive outboards—there was no way Rick would catch them. Before he could even tell Possum to research the name, Possum had some information.

"The boat is owned by a nonprofit organization called EnviroGents. They have received multiple grants from the government over the years, but none since November 2024," said Possum.

"What does EnviroGents do?" asked Rick.

"According to the mission statement on their website, they are dedicated to protecting ancestral lands and empowering Indigenous communities who steward them. It says, *We work to secure threatened territories, defend cultural heritage, and support sustainable practices that honor the deep connection between people and their environment. Through responsible advocacy, collaborative partnerships, and respectful engagement, our mission is to ensure that Indigenous lands remain protected, prosperous, and preserved for generations to come*," said Possum.

"I call bullshit. I bet you they are a money laundering NGO for some senator or congressman."

"Bingo. They received grant money from both parties. It all came to a grinding halt, though, when USAID was terminated."

"Good! I hate corruption!" Rick exclaimed. "How much you wanna bet they will be the highest bidder on Jake's land auction?"

"I ain't taking that bet. Look, there's Jules on her four-wheeler waving us over."

"Let's beach the cat and join them," Rick replied.

Rick dropped the stern anchor about thirty yards out and left it slack while he motored to the beach, lightly pushing the throttle to beach the cat on the sand. Possum tossed the forward anchor, and Gary picked it up, carrying it a few yards inland. Once both anchors were taut, Rick killed the engines.

"What are y'all doing on the boat?" Jules asked as they approached.

"Trying to catch a stalker. Someone in an Axopar boat was watching the beach house. Possum said it belongs to an NGO. I'm going to ask Carson to look into it. I have a gut feeling it's connected to the kidnapping."

"What are y'all up to?"

"We were just telling Gary how Jake loved camping out here. The story shifted to Malia never having a s'more. I guess they're not popular in Hawaii, so we went to the store while you were gone and picked up supplies. Gary's building a fire now. I texted you to join us when you got back. Didn't Possum tell you?"

"I'm sorry. I didn't see the text. When I got home, we hopped on the boat so fast that he didn't mention it. We were focused on trying to catch that boat," Rick confessed.

"Well, you're here now. Help me make s'mores!" Jules exclaimed.

Rick wasn't particularly keen on making s'mores, but he loved making Jules happy, so he got right to it. Gary had done a fantastic job on the fire, and Rick showed Malia how to brown a marshmallow without burning it. After a few attempts, Malia finally got it just right. They enjoyed a blast around the property, and before sunset, Rick and Possum took the catamaran back to the dock where Possum started dinner. Gary and the girls arrived fifteen minutes later.

While Possum worked in the kitchen, Rick called Carson

from the war room and filled him in on the stalker boat and the company that owned it. Carson said he would hit the pavement in D.C. to get details on the NGO.

As soon as Rick hung up, his phone rang. It was Jake.

"Hey, Jake. You still at the hospital?"

"Yeah, I think I'm heading out tonight, though. Listen, can you swing by my house? My security doorbell just pinged my phone. Someone dropped off a package, but they kept their face hidden. They weren't from FedEx or UPS," Jake explained.

"I'll go take a look. I'll call you back."

Rick asked Possum to come with him and to bring his pinpointer. Malia took over for Possum in the kitchen. When they arrived at Jake's house, a small box sat by the door. It had no postage, just one word: *Jake.*

"Could be a bomb," Rick cautioned.

"I kinda doubt it, but let's be careful nonetheless," Possum replied.

Possum used the pinpointer to check for metal inside. If there were plastic explosives, there might not be any firing mechanism. That would require some metal, at least, unless it had a chemical firing pin, which was uncommon and volatile. Rick decided there was only one way to find out. He jogged back to the Bronco and grabbed a spool of nylon string. Carefully, he made a noose around the box, running a hundred feet of line back toward the vehicle. He called Jake.

"Hey, buddy. We're here. Is anyone home at your place?"

"Let me check my cameras. Hang on," Jake said.

Rick waited a moment, and Jake returned.

"All clear. I can see you on the doorbell camera."

"Cool. You have good home insurance, right?" Rick asked.

"Replacement costs and then some—why?"

"We're about to find out. Just watch."

Rick pulled the line taut, took a deep breath, crouched behind the Bronco, and gave a huge yank on the string. The noose tightened around the box, flipping it through the air onto the grass.

"It ain't a bomb," Rick said, his heart racing.

"It could be poison or something like ricin or anthrax."

"I'll put on my mask just in case," Rick decided.

He rummaged through his Bronco for useful supplies, putting on his respirator and long rubber gloves. With a box cutter, he sliced through the tape sealing the box's flaps. As he slowly opened it, he found something wrapped in green face cloth. Carefully loosening the fabric, he revealed a severed ringed finger with a painted nail. Rick's stomach churned, and he fought the urge to vomit. The ring was distinctive, twisted like barbed wire in the center, either gold and silver or white gold and yellow gold.

"Jake, can you describe Cindy's ring?" Rick asked over the speaker, his voice steady but urgent.

"Why?"

"There's no easy way to say this, but there's a finger in the box."

"Oh shit. She wears a yellow-and-white gold ring twisted in the middle. I got it for her on a trip to Cozumel many years ago."

"I'm sorry. We'll have to run a DNA test on it to confirm, but it's likely to be hers. Do you have anything of hers we can get a DNA swab?"

"Check the top bathroom on the right side of the house. I'll unlock the door code for you. She has a blue and white battery-powered Oral-B toothbrush and a silver hairbrush in there."

Rick could hear Jake's voice crack—he was distraught, and rightly so. As soon as Jake unlocked the door, Rick and Possum headed upstairs to grab the items they needed from the bathroom. Possum bagged them up in an evidence bag, and they set off for FedEx. On the way, Possum called Carson.

"Hey Carson, Possum here. How quickly can you get me a DNA test for a finger against a couple of items from our kidnapped victim's belongings?"

"It will take a few days. I recommend you take it to the FDLE Tallahassee Crime Lab in Tallahassee. I can call ahead to inform them you're coming and encourage them to act quickly. DNA testing has advanced significantly since the 90s. If you go straight there, you might get a result by the end of tonight," Carson said.

"Wow, no kidding?"

"Yep, it depends on how good quality DNA you have. I'll call them now and I'll text you the address."

Possum ended the call, and his phone vibrated. He relayed the address to Rick, who drove quickly toward Tallahassee. They arrived in just over an hour. Inside the lab, the tech worked efficiently.

"If you guys wanna hang around, I can have results for you in an hour and a half," the technician said.

"We have to get back to Apalachicola. Can you just text me if it's a match?" Rick asked, handing the technician his card.

"No problem."

As they drove back, Possum studied the evidence.

"Why would they send her finger with no note?" he wondered.

"I don't know. Fear of the unknown?"

Suddenly, Rick's phone rang; it was Jake.

"What's up, Jake?"

"I just got an email from the kidnappers. I'll read it to you and then forward it to Possum."

Jake began to read, and Rick could hear the tension in his voice:

"Jake,

We've been very patient with you, but our patience is running out. If you don't surrender your land by tomorrow, you'll receive Cindy in several boxes, one body part at a time. Create a Charitable Remainder Trust (CRT) in the name of JBC LLC and have the paperwork hand-delivered to Queensgate Bank and Trust Company Ltd. in Grand Cayman no later than 5:00 p.m. tomorrow.

CJ"

"Is that even possible?" asked Jake, panic rising.

"Yes, it's possible. I'm not flying to Grand Cayman; I'm pretty sure there's still a warrant for my arrest there. But we can have Gary rent a private jet to take it. Do you have a lawyer in town who can create the documents?"

"Yes. I'll call him to get started. I don't even want the land anymore; I just want Cindy back," Jake replied, filled with desperation.

"Okay, call him and send me his address. I'll call Gary and have him arrange the jet. I understand your dilemma. If I can come up with another plan, I will. Otherwise, we can fetch Cindy back and handle it in court. My guess is the land will be transferred to various corporations in offshore accounts and then legitimately sold to whoever wants it. It won't be easy to trace or prosecute, but it's doable. Call me back after you talk to your lawyer."

Rick quickly called Gary, asking him to prepare a jet for Cayman. He kept driving toward the beach house, wrestling with how to save the land and rescue Cindy simultaneously. He knew Jake was willing to give up the land to save his daughter, but Rick felt convinced there had to be another way.

As they neared Apalachicola city limits, Rick received a text from a 448 area code, which was used in Tallahassee. It contained only two words:

No Match!

"Fuckin' A! It's not Cindy's finger. Possum, call the morgue and see if there are any women's bodies there with missing fingers."

"I'm on it. Are you gonna let Jake know?"

"Not yet. I want him to still believe it's Cindy's. That way, if he has to talk to the kidnappers, his emotions will seem genuine. I have a plan. Can you copy the CRT Jake's lawyer is working on but change it enough so it's not binding?"

"Since Jake is under duress, in the hospital, and still believes the kidnappers cut off her finger, we can use the Unanticipated Events Clause: major life changes or cases where the beneficiary no longer wants payments, which require court-approved termination. The bank will take control of it, but it will automatically be revoked because ownership has been transferred. It will be a worthless piece of paper."

"Brilliant! I'm sure the kidnappers know we'll do a DNA test on the finger, but they have no idea we already have the results. They probably think it will take a few days. Just enough time to do the land giveaway," said Rick.

"What about the auction?" asked Possum.

"There's no need for it now. I'll swing by and let Gabe know. There's no need for him to waste any more time on that now. Then we can pick up the paperwork for the CRT from Jake's lawyer. The address isn't far from Gabe's."

Rick pulled into the parking lot of Gabe's office and walked to the door. There were no cars parked outside, but Jake had told Rick that Gabe would be working late into the night. He knocked on the door, but the lights were off. He cupped his hands against the glass and peered inside. It was empty—barren, with only a dusty old wood floor visible.

"What the fuck?"

Possum was on the phone, speaking just out of Rick's earshot to someone.

"Rick, we need to go to the morgue. A homeless woman who died has a missing finger. There are surveillance cameras. The security guard called the police, but they won't be there for a bit. Let's see if we can take a look at that footage before they do."

They quickly jumped into the Bronco and headed toward the morgue, arriving in ten minutes. Since Apalachicola was small, it didn't have a dedicated morgue; Kelly Funeral Home handled all human remains. When they reached the funeral home, it was easy to convince the security guard to show them the surveillance footage. Possum flashed a shiny badge he'd received in Canada from the Special Investigative Unit as a CSIS liaison, and the guard fell for it.

As they scrolled back through the footage, they both gasped at what they saw. A video showed a man entering the cold room after hours.

"Gabe?!" they exclaimed simultaneously.

They watched intently as it became painfully evident that Gabe was nervous. He donned latex gloves, wiped sweat from his forehead with his shirt sleeve, then pulled out tin snips and cut off the woman's ring finger, nearly vomiting as he shook. After placing the ring on the severed limb, he wrapped it in a green face cloth and exited through the back door.

Rick and Possum exchanged a stunned silence. After a moment, Possum had the security guard make him a DVD copy of the footage, and they made their way out, already plotting their next move.

CHAPTER
SEVEN

There was still glistening dew on the tarmac as the pilot taxied down the Tallahassee runway. Gary and Kelly fastened their seat belts and prepared for take-off, holding hands as the nose lifted and they became airborne. Rick had loaned Gary his Meta Ray-Ban sunglasses, which had recording capability; he'd blacked out the flashing white light that indicated recording. The glasses featured transition lenses, allowing Gary to sync them to a live feed on Facebook or Instagram. Rick had set up a private page for them to watch along. There was no way he was setting foot in Grand Cayman.

Possum had altered the original CRT document just enough to render it invalid; it would take days for the bank in Grand Cayman to realize what had happened. Jake was unaware of Rick and Possum's plan—he was prepared to give up his land to save his daughter, but Rick would let him know when the time was right. For now, he had to keep it to himself.

The plane landed in Grand Cayman just before 10:00 a.m. Kelly looked stunning, dressed to the nines alongside Gary, who was playing the role of a sophisticated land broker. One significant change Possum made to the document was substituting Jake's lawyer's name for Gary Haas. While Gary was not a lawyer, he had all the right IDs and an online presence that could fool the most inquisitive broker. Possum, a skilled dark web hacker, had crafted an impressive profile for Gary.

"You ready to do this, Kelly?" Gary asked, full of charm.

"I am. Do I call you Mr. Hass, Gary Haas, Esquire, or what?"

"Call me whatever you want, just don't call me late for a beer," he quipped, his Texas drawl evident.

Despite being a multimillionaire, Gary was a true redneck through and through. He could charm even the staunchest businessman, though he appeared an unvarnished operator. Yet today, he would be suave and collected as they entered the posh bank to meet the branch manager.

"Good afternoon, Mr. Haas. I am Mr. Bernal Smythe, branch manager. Are you ready to proceed with the CRT?"

"I am indeed. Miss Broussard, you have the documents?"

Kelly reached into her briefcase and produced a folder.

It was strange hearing Gary call her by her maiden name, as she was now a Haas in every practical sense.

Kelly passed the folder to Mr. Smythe, who examined it closely, raising an eyebrow. Both Gary and Kelly held their breath.

"It all looks good. Let me get this notarized and make you some copies. Once it's delivered to the courthouse, it will be valid. Can I email you the government-stamped documents in a day or so?" Mr. Smythe asked.

"That would be fine. Here's my card," Gary replied. "If we're done here, I have other businesses to attend to."

"Very well. Have a nice day, and thank you for choosing Queensgate Bank and Trust Company, Ltd." Gary shook his hand, and Rick and the gang watched the transaction unfold on a private Facebook page.

Once outside, Gary spoke quietly to the crew watching through his Meta Ray-Bans.

"How'd we do, Rick? We earn a beer?"

It was a one-way conversation, but Gary knew they were listening. As soon as he got back to the car, he flipped the glasses around, aiming the camera at his face.

"Did we do good or what?! We're gonna head over to Lone Star Bar & Grill. I'll have one of those Cadillac margaritas for ya, Rick!" he exclaimed with a hearty laugh.

He was just teasing Rick; Gary didn't really want to go to that bar. Besides, he had a cooler full of Busch Light tallboys on ice in the jet. As hot as Kelly looked in that dress, he hoped to join the mile-high club on the return flight.

With only two pilots on the flight and no flight attendants, Gary had tipped them generously and instructed them to stay in the cockpit, allowing him and Kelly some privacy. The flight took off before noon, and it wasn't long before they slipped into the lounge area, closing the curtain behind them. They were still considered newlyweds, after all.

Meanwhile, Rick and Jules headed to Jake's house to give Possum and Malia some privacy. They hadn't had any time alone since arriving. It was a necessary trip because Jake was now home, and Rick wanted to check on his physical and mental well-being. The betrayal he felt from Gabe's involvement in Cindy's disappearance weighed heavily on his mind—Jake had been with his firm for years.

"Knock, knock," Rick said sarcastically to the doorbell camera as Jake buzzed them in.

"How are you feeling, Jake?"

"Betrayed. But with a headache."

"Head still hurting, huh?" Rick asked.

"Yeah, but my heart hurts more. I can't believe Gabe was involved in this plan. Are you sure?"

"I'm sure, but there's more to the story. Please bear with me. I can't tell you everything just yet."

"What do you mean?"

"You're just gonna have to trust me, Jake. I have Cindy's best interest at heart."

Rick explained that he believed it was Gabe who had delivered Cindy's ring finger in a box, intentionally omitting the fact that it wasn't actually Cindy's finger. He needed Jake to believe it was; otherwise, there was a chance he wouldn't proceed with transferring ownership of the land. Jake looked defeated yet hopeful. The kidnappers had said they would return Cindy by 6:00 p.m. if Jake followed through with his promise. It was now 5:30 p.m., and they said they would call with her location on the hour.

"Are you nervous?" Rick asked.

"Yeah, I ain't gonna lie. What if they kill her? What's to stop them now?"

"Just keep the faith. It's gonna happen. I feel good about her safe return tonight."

Jake paced, glancing at his watch.

"Fuck, it's 6:03 p.m.! Why haven't they called or texted?!"

Before he could finish, his phone vibrated.

Oystertown Books – Rooftop.

Jake showed Rick the screen, determination taking over his anxiety.

"Let's roll."

Jules drove shotgun as Rick raced downtown. He parked in front of the little bookstore, which now had new owners and a new name. They rushed down the alley to the back, where a built-in wall ladder awaited. Rick, packing his gear, climbed first, while Jules stayed on the ground to keep watch as Jake followed him up the ladder.

On the roof, Rick scanned the area and saw a lone figure in the center, slumped in a chair.

"Come on up, Jake."

Jake climbed up, and upon seeing the figure, he rushed forward. It was Cindy, slumped over with her long hair in a ponytail, draped in a colorful Mexican poncho that concealed her hands.

"Cindy... baby, are you alright?" he asked, dropping to his knees.

"Yes, I'm okay. I'm tied up. Please take me home," she replied, her voice quivering.

Jake pulled back the poncho, expecting to see her right hand wrapped in gauze. Instead, she had all her fingers intact.

"That's the part I couldn't tell you. It'll all make sense when we get home. I'll tell you the rest of it as well," said, relieved but anxious.

"Cindy, this is Rick Waters. He and his team are the main reason you are free," Jake introduced, pride swelling in his chest.

"Thank you, Mr. Waters," Cindy murmured.

"Call me Rick. I can't wait for you to meet my wife, Jules. She's in the back of the building watching our six. Y'all are gonna hit it off.

A faint smile graced Cindy's face as Rick cut the ropes binding her, and Jake helped get her to the ladder.

"Are you strong enough to climb down?" Rick asked, concern etched on his face.

"Yes, they kept me fed and hydrated pretty well. I'm just mentally drained," she replied.

Jake climbed down a bit to be ready if she stumbled. Rick kept vigilant, scanning the rooftops and the street below. They safely made it down, and Rick rushed them into the Bronco, speeding off toward St. George Island.

As they arrived, they spotted two deputy sheriff cruisers parked out front of Jake's property. One was taking a statement from Cindy, the other there for protection. There would be a cruiser stationed 24/7 for a few days.

Once the deputy took his statement, Cindy took a long shower. When she emerged, she looked significantly better than she had on the roof. The four of them gathered in the great room, and Rick filled Jake in on everything. He was amazed at what they had pulled off.

"So, it's over?" Jake asked, hope flickering in his eyes.

"Not exactly, Jake. It's really only just started. Once whoever is the kingpin of this operation finds out that the land trust documents were forged and that Kelly Broussard is not a lawyer, shit's gonna hit the fan. They're gonna come at you with revenge in their veins. So, how about a bit of vacation? I'm seriously gonna want to be home, Cindy, but until we nail these guys, your lives are in danger. Have you ever been to Cuba?"

"Cuba? Why Cuba?"

"Because it's the last place they'll ever think to look for you. My partner, Gary, owns a massive nursery there, and it's like a damn fortress. Gary landed in Tallahassee, and they are waiting for you. He and Kelly will fly you two there to stay at the safe house. You're gonna love it. It's incredibly lush and is surrounded by all sorts of beautiful wildlife. If you can pack, we can take you tonight. If you're too exhausted, we can leave in the morning. It will take a day or two for the bank to figure out what we did with the documents."

"If it's okay, we'd prefer to leave in the morning. The cop will be outside, right?"

"Yes, that's fine. I'll call you after breakfast. Gary and Kelly will probably just get a room in Tallahassee. They are still newlyweds, you know?"

"Thanks, Rick. Cindy and I have some father-daughter catching up to do."

"I totally understand. We'll leave you to it."

Rick shook hands with Jake and Cindy, while Jules embraced them both. Cindy appeared to melt into Jules' gentle presence—a soft balm after her harrowing experience.

Rick and Jules left, heading back to the beach house. He called Gary to relay the plan, and Gary confirmed he'd get a room near the airport and wait for Jake and Cindy to arrive in the morning.

When Rick and Jules reached the beach house, they were greeted by a celebratory feast set up by Possum and Malia. The spread resembled a luau rather than a typical dinner. Jules had kept Malia updated through texts about Cindy.

"We did it, Rick! How's Cindy?" Possum asked.

"She is surprisingly good. Gary and Kelly will fly them to the nursery grounds in Cuba in the morning. That's a great safe house for them."

"Ah, Cuba. Good call. There's no doubt whoever is in charge will be furious once they find out the land doesn't belong to them and Cindy is free."

"I'm hoping their anger will cause them to slip up," Rick replied.

"That's a good point. We'll have targets on us as well."

"We already do, hombre. We already do."

"I guess you're right, Rick."

"As far as we know, they aren't murderers. At least not yet. Kidnappers and thieves, yes, murderers, no."

"We best not give them a chance to upgrade. We have a day or so until they figure it out. I say we have Johnie bring up Possum's Bronco and take the catamaran back to Destin, and we take up residence in Jake's place. That will be ground zero. Let's keep them guessing."

"We can use Jake's Suburban. It has tinted windows, and he keeps it in the garage."

"What about the motorhome?"

"I'll hire a driver to take it back to Destin with the Bronco in tow. They'll think we left now that Cindy's home."

"Great idea. Let's eat."

Rick cracked open a Collective Arts Hazy IPA for himself and an Athletic Upside Dawn for Jules. He ran to his room to grab his Buzz Drops, dispensing a few squeezes for himself. Malia made Mai Tais for her and Possum, and they clinked glasses, toasted to Cindy's safe return. They cheered until around ten o'clock when exhaustion set in, and they called it a night.

The next morning, after breakfast , Rick texted Jake.

Y'all packed and ready?

Yes, sir. We talked it over and are looking forward to a getaway now.

Rick called and arranged for a driver. He and Jules rode their bikes over to Jake's and parked them in the garage. They all planned to head to Tallahassee in Jake's Suburban. Rick texted Johnie, asking if he could drive Possum's Bronco to

Apalachicola to deliver the catamaran back to Destin, then called a delivery service to take the motorhome back as well. He told Johnie to put the Italian plates from Rick's Ferrari on the Bronco—completely untraceable. The disappearing act was in full swing; they wanted whoever initiated the kidnapping to believe the crew had given up on the case.

As they entered the garage, Jules tied her hair in a ponytail and donned some of Cindy's clothes.

"I hate to do this to you, mate, but I need your signature hat," Rick said, eyeing Jake's bright orange baseball cap, emblazoned with a black Browning deer silhouette logo.

Jake willingly handed it over. Rick had shaved his goatee and temporarily darkened his hair. They would be impersonating Cindy and Jake for the foreseeable future.

Once they loaded up the Suburban, they headed to the Tallahassee airport. Cindy and Jake ducked down in the back seat until they were out of town.

"How did you two meet?" Cindy asked, feeling lighter, her spirits lifting with each passing moment.

"I was a dealer in St. Croix," Gary said with a smile. "Rick approached the craps table. I noticed him checking me out as soon as he took his seat. Later, I bumped into him at a local restaurant bar I frequented for a nightcap after my shift. He bought me a drink and swept me off my feet."

"That is so sweet," Cindy replied, warmth radiating from her.

"Do you have anyone special in your life, Cindy?" Jules asked, catching the mood.

"I did. I was engaged, but I called it off. Too many red flags. I've been so focused on getting our brewery off the ground that I haven't been dating. I'm not opposed to it. It's just not the right time."

"I understand. When the time is right, you will know," Jules said, a comforting hand on Cindy's shoulder.

Jules and Cindy chatted all the way to the airport. When they arrived, Rick introduced them to Gary and Kelly, and they loaded their luggage onto the jet, exchanging hugs and heartfelt goodbyes.

"Y'all have fun in Cuba. It's a land of many contrasting things: wealth and poverty, growth and decline, civilization and the great wild. You're gonna love it. When y'all return, we should have the person who did this in custody. I can keep you posted via Zoom calls. I may have questions that pop up. Oh yeah, I almost forgot. Take these burner phones. Gary will get you Cuban SIM cards. As I mentioned, I'll use your phones and keep them with us at all times. Jules and I will communicate using your phones back at your house. I know it must feel a little uncomfortable giving me your passwords but the longer we can make them think that we are you two, the better. It's the master plan," Rick explained.

"I don't care at all, Rick. There's nothing on my phone I'm ashamed of."

"Haha, I hear ya. Well, have a safe flight, and we can communicate via the burner phones and Zoom. It's a highly encrypted program that Possum downloaded from the dark web. He will send you a link."

They boarded the private jet, Rick and Jules waving as it taxied down the tarmac.

Returning to the Suburban, Rick and Jules drove back to Jake's place, now ready to start their impersonation as Jake and Cindy for as long as necessary. He had instructed Johnie to bring along Rick's two battle boxes—his flight cases full of weapons, ammo, explosives, and everything they might need for protection or a prolonged standoff.

CHAPTER
EIGHT

Possum and Malia had rented a small condo on the other side of St. George Island, while Jake's beach house, where their group had initially stayed, now sat empty. Before leaving, Possum installed several hidden cameras around the property to catch any potential stalkers. The cameras were motion-activated and linked to his laptop. Rick made it a point never to meet Possum at either Jake's house or the new condo; all communications would be highly encrypted. They agreed to meet in a concealed location just outside St. George Island and Apalachicola.

Jake also provided Rick with a punch list of tasks needed at the Brew Pub to keep their cover story intact, and Jules, who loved organizing, took it to heart. In addition to taking down the bad guys, she was eager to ensure an amazing grand opening when the time was right.

The first few days were quiet. No one visited Jake's place or the beach house the group rented. Everything changed on day three when Jake received an email revealing that the land CRT contract Gary had delivered to Grand Cayman was a forgery. The contract was now officially null and void. The bank desperately tried to contact Jake, and the phone he left at his beach house kept ringing nonstop. Rick, of course, never answered it and knew that the kidnappers now realized they had been double-crossed. A reckoning is coming, and Rick couldn't be happier about it. At midnight, a dark car circled Jake's beach house and slowed down several times. It also drove past the beachhouse and stopped in front of it. A man in black sweats and a hoodie crept up to the front door and peeked inside. His face was covered, so Possum pressed a button to make the camera beep, and when he looked up to see where the noise was coming from, Possum got a full view of his face. He immediately recognized him as the Indian guy from the FLDE sketch. They had no idea what his name was, so Possum forwarded the still shot to Carson to run it through his facial recognition software in Quantico. The FBI's forensic research lab was the world's most state-of-the-art facility. If the guy had ever had his photo taken for any government ID, he would be identified.

Possum texted Rick on the burner phone to meet him in the morning at a pin he saved on Google Maps. It was down a park ranger road in the heart of the Apalachicola National Forest—a perfect spot for a secret meetup.

Rick picked up supplies from Jake's task list at a supplier in Apalachicola and dropped Jules and the goods off at the new Brew Pub location. He hesitated about leaving her alone, but she insisted she'd be fine. To ease his mind, he made her wear a bulletproof vest beneath a loose blouse. She was heavily armed and fully capable of handling herself, given her experience managing tap lines at a restaurant she had helped design in Colombia.

Rick drove the Suburban into town, parked, and switched cars, renting one that wouldn't stand out. He donned his Sunbody fine palm cowboy hat, removed his camp shirt to reveal a white T-shirt, and swapped his thick shades for a more nondescript pair as he walked toward the rental car. His transformation from Jake to Rick had taken less than fifteen steps.

As he arrived at the canopied clearing, he spotted Possum lounging on the hood of a rental car.

"Hey, hombre. We hit a break in the case. Carson identified the guy from the sketch artist's drawing. His name is Dakota Catawanee. He's got a rap sheet as long as your arm," Possum shared, his expression serious.

"Do you think he is the mastermind?"

"No way. He is just the muscle. He's not smart enough. Carson took it upon himself to do a forensic accounting of his bank. He's received several large payments from an offshore company over the past two months. The first one was a few days before Cindy was kidnapped. The last one was a few days ago. In fact, it was a huge payout and was the same day Gary flew to Grand Cayman. Coincidence? I think not. This thing goes deep. I think there is a government connection that is tied to one of the energy companies."

"You mean like Exxon or Chevron?"

"I'm not saying them in particular, but definitely one of the big ones."

"That means they have deep pockets. How are we gonna go up against them?" Rick asked, concern etching his brow.

"One day at a time, my friend. One day at a time."

Possum handed Rick a flash drive containing all the intel he had on Dakota Catawanee. He was a tough character—having served time at the Northwest Florida Reception Center (known locally as the Chipley Chalet) for assault and attempted kidnapping. He'd been released early due to overcrowding during the COVID era and was currently on parole. The only job on his record was as a part-time barback at a local pub—definitely not enough to explain the large sums of money in his bank account.

Taking him down wouldn't be tricky, but Rick wanted the top guy behind the operation. If he could get Dakota to flip in exchange for testifying, it could change everything. First, he had to locate him, and his best bet was where Dakota worked —the High Five Dive Bar on Commerce Street in downtown Apalachicola. Rick planned to case the bar later that night.

He returned to the rental car, got behind the wheel of the Suburban, and headed back to where Jules was working. Upon arrival, he found her knee-deep in setting up the glycol draft beer system at the Brew Pub. The setup, featuring a large cooler supplying glycol-cooled lines to the tap handles, was brilliant. Most impressively, all the draft beer lines were concealed within a faux ceiling panel, with invisible hinges for easy access.

"You sure you aren't a contractor?" Rick joked.

"I probably could've been in a different life. I can build just about anything. I was a tomboy and learned everything I know by following my dad around," she replied, fingers deftly working.

"Color me impressed. Let me lend a hand."

Rick filled Jules in on the case as they continued working on the glycol lines. By the time darkness fell outside, they had finished half of the lines—a significant accomplishment.

"What's the plan tonight?" Jules asked, wiping her brow.

"We're gonna commit it as a kidnapping. I could use a diversion. You in?"

"Do chickens cross the road to get the early worm?" she replied, a playful twinkle in her eye.

"Uh..." Rick began, but he decided to let her mix metaphors.

"Okay, do you have your Valentina outfit?"

"You know I do," she grinned.

The Valentina outfit consisted of a long black dress with a slit up the side, a curly auburn wig, and exaggerated makeup. The transformation was so convincing that it had become one of her signature personas, originally inspired on the fly by one of her favorite hot sauces during a previous case in Destin. Jules had invented the 'New Rican' accent, a blend of New York and Puerto Rican, and she nailed it every time.

They headed to Jake's place, where Jules prepared her outfit and makeup kit. She packed everything into a duffel bag, and they left the house in the Suburban. After quickly switching vehicles, they headed to a rented hotel room. Jules began her transformation while Rick waited in bed, checking his weapons, including a tranquilizer gun.

Possum had concocted a mix of fentanyl, lorazepam, and propofol, dubbing it the "Michael Jackson cocktail." Sadly, it was the same mix that had led to the pop star's early death. Additionally, he had devised a wrist-mounted tranquilizer gun that looked like Spiderman shooting web from his wrist. It was incredibly accurate and effective.

Meanwhile, Carson was assembling a team of special agents just outside of town. They were set to use unique interrogation techniques that Rick recognized all too well. Was it legal? Probably not, but if it took down a big fish, it would be worth it. Rick dropped Jules off a block from the bar and parked behind a dumpster for cover. He figured if

Jules could entice Dakota outside for a smoke, he could nab him.

The bar was alive with energy when Jules entered. She turned heads all around, even from women in the room. Sitting alone at a table, every man tried to buy her a drink, which she gracefully declined while ordering her own from a waitress. She focused on Dakota, who was behind the bar, stacking beer boxes like a true busboy.

"Hi, beautiful night," Jules started as he cleared a table nearby.

"Yes, ma'am. It sure is," Dakota replied, busily putting glasses in a bus tub.

He moved away, and she sipped her soda, making small talk each time he came by to clear tables.

"What's your name?" she inquired.

"I'm Dakota, ma'am."

He was surprisingly respectful for a kidnapper.

"Dakota, that's a unique name. I'm Valentina," she said, tossing her hair.

"It's native. Valentina is unique as well."

"Yes, I'm Puerto Rican. I think my mom named me after hot sauce." They both laughed, the tension easing.

"You look like you're a man of means. You smoke?" she asked, mimicking a joint with her hand.

He glanced around, as if cautious of being watched.

"I get a break in a few minutes. Follow me out back; I got a fatty."

"Now you're talking!"

Dakota cleaned a few glasses and stocked some more beer, then walked outside and nodded his head a little. Jules waited until he turned the corner and texted Rick as she walked out.

Get ready.

Dakota posted up behind the dumpster, and Rick had a clear view of him from the shadows. Jules walked up just as Dakota lit the joint. Rick moved forward behind Dakota and fired the tranquilizer dart. In one motion, he reached back as if to swat a bee sting and then fell to his knees. He was out cold. Jules helped Rick drag him to the car, and they put him in the trunk. They drove off to the meetup point with the special agents. As they got close, Rick could hear noise coming from the trunk.

"He's waking up," said Jules.

"Good!" replied Rick as he slipped on a pair of brass knuckles.

When they arrived at the location, a black, dark-tinted SUV was parked on a side road. Rick stopped the car and stepped out. He took a deep breath and quickly opened the trunk. Dakota lunged toward Rick and Rick hit him squarely in the nose, knocking him out again.

"That one's for Cindy!"

He pulled his limp body out of the trunk, and two men in suits slipped on flex cuffs on his wrists and ankles, then threw him in the back of the SUV. They sped off within seconds without a single word spoken. Rick had a feeling Dakota would be joining Jake and Cindy on the island of Cuba, but at a different location—Guantanamo.

Rick and Jules, aka Valentine, drove back to the hotel. They slipped inside and resumed their Jake and Cindy identities, parked the rental car, and took the Suburban back to Jake's beach house. Step one was complete.

Gunfire erupted , waking Rick and Jules from a deep sleep. They dove for cover in the bathroom as bullets riddled the front door and shattered the windows of the beach house. The assailants were using silencers and automatic weapons, and just as suddenly as it began, the shooting stopped. Rick sprinted to the upstairs window and caught a glimpse of a dark sedan speeding off.

Clearly, this wasn't a random attack; it was a warning, as the shooters would have targeted the upstairs bedrooms if their goal had been lethality. All of Jake's properties had massive great rooms, kitchens, and offices downstairs, with bedrooms located upstairs—a well-thought-out design.

Rick dashed downstairs with his weapon drawn, scanning for threats. The front door had been obliterated, and a rock lay at the threshold, attached to a note. Donning latex gloves, he picked up the rock and read the note.

Nice try, Jake. That wasn't very kind. We had a deal, and you broke it. We want the land, and we WILL get it.

— CJ

In the morning, Rick would send the note and rock to Quantico to see if Carson could extract a DNA profile. They couldn't stay overnight, so he quickly packed a go-bag, and they headed into town for the rental car. They switched vehicles and returned to the hotel room he had rented earlier.

"What are we gonna do, Rick?"

I'm gonna call Jake and have him contact the police. I'll tell him to say he's hiding nearby for his own safety. The local police will conduct an investigation of the shooting, but it probably won't go anywhere. It will at least look like Jake is on top of it and whoever is responsible will still think he's home.

By the time they wrapped up all of that, it was nearly 4:00

a.m. when Rick and Jules finally settled back into sleep. A little love-making session had helped them relax.

~

Rick brewed coffee as Jules drifted out of sleep. He had already called an out-of-town contractor to meet at the crime scene. Rick wanted an estimate to replace the damaged windows and front door as soon as possible. Once they agreed on a price, he asked if he could order the supplies and get it done as soon as the police released the residence, offering to pay double.

The contractor left, and Rick called Jake to check on the police situation. They told him that since no one was injured, they would check surveillance video to investigate, but he was free to return to his home. The contractor returned at 1:30 p.m. and immediately got to work, replacing the front door and all the busted windows. Despite the surrounding chaos, the beach house began to look functional again.

It was functionally repaired, and they said they would come back the next day to do aesthetic work and paint. Rick always thought it was amazing what a good contractor could do if paid well. Rick forwarded the surveillance video he'd captured of the sedan to Possum and brought him up to speed. He told Rick he'd study it and see what he could come up with.

~

Later, Rick received a message from Carson. The rock and note didn't match anyone in the CODIS database or Dakota's profile, who was currently in custody somewhere and being thoroughly interrogated. Rick and Jules spent the day solidifying their Jake and Cindy personas. They worked on the Brew Pub until dinner time, but rather than risk discovery by eating out, they ordered delivery from Hong Kong Bistro.

Although Jules wasn't a fan of Chinese food due to the MSG, she made sure to hydrate well. As they settled into their roles, they were growing weary of pretending to be Jake and Cindy, but they knew it was necessary.

Once they returned to Jake's house, closed the curtains, and changed back, they showered and enjoyed some quality time together.

"Wanna watch a movie?" Jules asked, stretching luxuriously.

"Sure. Whatcha got in mind?"

"How about that movie *Coda*? It's about a deaf girl who struggles between following her dreams to go to Berkeley or staying at home to help with the family fishing business. Sounds inspiring."

"I could use a little inspiration. Let's do it," Rick agreed.

The movie, rated 8.0 on IMDb, met and exceeded expectations. Rick didn't usually lean toward feel-good films, but after having binged every episode of *Dateline* and *Forensic Files* more times than he could count, he welcomed a break from violence and negativity.

After watching the heartwarming film, they felt genuinely uplifted.

Before bed, they enjoyed a long soak in the hot tub. One neck massage led to another, which culminated in a beautiful love-making session—a perfect ending to an unexpectedly sweet day. They fell asleep in each other's arms, feeling snug and safe all night long.

CHAPTER
NINE

Rick's burner phone began vibrating at 8:12 a.m. He picked it up and answered.

"Hello, Jake. How's Cuba?"

"Hi, Rick. You were right. This place is amazing. We love the wildlife and the peace and quiet of the nursery. We had a late-night talk, and Cindy remembered something that might be helpful. I did too, but I'll let you talk to her first."

"Hi, Rick," Cindy's voice came through the line.

"Hi, Cindy. You're on speaker with Jules."

"Hi, Jules."

"Hi, Cindy! We're glad you're enjoying Cuba."

"We really are. Listen, I remember something from last night that happened during the day while the kidnappers were talking on the phone. I could hear a gravelly voice through the phone, and the guy was furious. He was making demands and yelling. I couldn't make out the words, but his voice was definitely scratchy and rough, similar to how Gavin Newsom sounds when he speaks. It wasn't Gavin, of course, but the man's voice had a similar quality. Then the kidnapper said, and I quote, 'There is no way you can't win a seat in FL-1 district 3, Gaetz already stepped down anyway. Not a chance. Stop worrying,' and then he ended the call."

"Wow, that means whoever the kidnapper was talking to is running for the vacant seat left when Matt Gaetz stepped down to become the U.S. Attorney General. I wonder how many candidates are in that race. Whoever wins the primary in that district will likely secure the seat because it leans +18 for the Republicans. I also wonder if that candidate needs the campaign funding. This could be a major development. Great job, Cindy."

"Rick, Jake here. Call Chuck Asbury. He's a first-time candidate and a good guy. I can assure you he's not involved, but he and his team probably have all the details about the other candidates and might know if one of them is corrupt. I'll text his number to you once we hang up."

"Thanks, Jake. You said you also remembered something?"

"Yeah, I started wondering. What if it's not the oil, natural gas, and rare earth minerals they're after? What if, instead of it being something they want to extract from the ground, it's something they want to keep in the ground?"

"Like what?"

"I don't know, but it might be worth pursuing. Just add it to the list of possibilities."

"Will do, Jake. If y'all think of anything else, let me know."

After hanging up, Rick's burner phone vibrated again. He quickly called Chuck and left a message. Less than five minutes later, Chuck called back.

"Mr. Waters, I got your message. You said you're friends with Jake Richmond. How can I help?"

"Yes, thanks for calling me back, Mr. Asbury. Call me Rick."

"Call me Chuck."

"Thanks, Chuck. Jake told me you're running for an open seat in the next Republican primary. He said you might have some details on the other candidates. Is there anything odd or possibly corrupt about any of them that stands out?"

"Off the record, and you didn't hear this from me, but it was in public records and has since been expunged—one of the candidates, Vito Profaci, was investigated for human trafficking a few years ago. However, the case was dropped because all the witnesses disappeared—like off the face of the planet. He's originally from New Jersey and is rumored to have ties to a crime family there. He has no convictions, and all charges were dismissed and subsequently expunged. So it's off-limits to the media."

"Does he by chance have a raspy voice?"

"He does. How did you know?"

"Someone told me something that made me believe that. Thank you so much for the information. I'll keep it to myself. We never met. Good luck with your campaign. If I can help in any way, don't hesitate to ask."

"Thank you, Rick. I might end up taking you up on that."

"Please do."

"That was a great call. I think Jake was onto something. I'm gonna have Possum put all his search efforts into finding out everything he can on this Vito guy. Sounds like a crooked nose," Rick noted.

"Really? I hope it leads somewhere," Jules remarked.

"Me too. I'm gonna call Possum and have him find out everything he can about Vito Profaci."

"I'll make us some coffee," Jules offered, heading to the kitchen.

Rick texted Possum on the burner phone, and he called back immediately.

"What's up, Rick?"

"Can you find out everything you can about Vito Profaci? I think he's linked to organized crime in New Jersey, and he's one of the candidates for that upcoming congressional position in District 3."

"You think he's involved with the kidnapping?" Possum asked.

"I do. I have a gut feeling I'm onto something."

Jules returned a few minutes later with coffee for Rick. He took a sip as Jules gestured like she was riding a bike. Rick nodded, and once he hung up, they changed and headed to Jake's oversized garage next to the beach house. The garage was separate from the one housing the Suburban, and Rick was astonished at all the toys Jake had collected.

There were two of everything—obviously for him and his daughter. Rick had promised Jules he'd teach her how to ride a wheelie, and although they'd have to disguise themselves as Jake and Cindy, it would be simple. On the wall hung off-road riding gear, complete with custom designs that featured their names and the Forgotten Coast Brewing Company Race Team logo on all the apparel. Even the matching Yamaha YZ 125 dirt bikes displayed the FCBC emblem.

Sporting helmets, both Rick and Jules concealed their pistols under their riding gear, knowing they were being watched. Rick took Jake's signature orange baseball cap while Jules swept her hair into a ponytail and donned oversized dark shades to mask her identity. As Rick raised the garage door, they blasted onto the street, headed for the vacant land Jake owned.

When they arrived, Rick instructed Jules on popping the

clutch to raise the front wheel of the bike. She practiced until she finally managed to wheelie—though the first few attempts ended in flipping over. Rick chose a soft-sand spot for her final attempts, where the ground was forgiving. On Jules' fifth try, she kept the front wheel off the ground for nearly twenty yards.

"Woo-hoo!" she cheered as she skidded to a stop.

As she climbed off her motorcycle, she noticed a blue nylon cord tied to a stick protruding from the sand. She tugged on the cord, which popped free, revealing a skull.

"Oh my God, Rick. Look!"

Rick glanced down, spotting the half-buried skull. His instincts kicked in, and he scanned the area for onlookers. He marked the spot on his phone's GPS and quickly covered the skull with loose sand.

"We need to leave. What do we do now?" asked Jules, urgency lacing her voice.

"We call Carson. That's definitely a ligature, and it must've been wrapped around the neck of whoever's skull this is. The FBI doesn't have jurisdiction here unless the body came from across state lines. I don't want to involve local police yet. There might be a mole on the inside. If Carson can get a team down here to identify the body and determine where it came from, they can take the case. Maybe that's why they wanted to acquire the land—not to dig something up, but to keep it buried."

Rick relayed the details of the scene to Carson and sent him the GPS coordinates. Carson confirmed he could have a forensic team from Tallahassee there that night. They would be discreet and equipped with night vision to exhume the body.

"Rick, can you take them to the site? You'll have to hike in under the cover of darkness," Carson instructed.

"Yeah, please send them to this address. I'll meet them there, and we can go over the plan."

Rick planned to book adjoining rooms at a small hotel in Apalachicola for the team's arrival.

"What do you want for lunch?" Jules queried.

"Just something easy. You pick," he replied, confident she would opt for something healthy, as always.

He went to the war room, called Possum, and filled him in on their discovery.

"I have a bad feeling about this, Rick. We may be in over our heads. I noticed someone canvassing the house we are in last night. I don't feel safe here. I'm worried about Malia," Possum admitted.

"Okay, I understand. Look, safety is in numbers. As soon as it's dark, head over here in an Uber. Have them drop you off at the house next door, then walk around the back. I'll let you in through the sliding glass doors. You all can stay with us. I have a virtual arsenal at the ready," Rick assured him.

"Okay. I'll be there around 6:30 p.m."

"Perfect. I'm meeting some Feds in town at 8:00 p.m. We're heading out on a little scavenger hunt. You can stay with Malia and Jules, guarding the house while I'm gone. Do you think we need to bring in some private security?"

"I'm not sure yet. But with you two pretending to be Jake and Cindy, you have targets on your back. We should consider it."

"If we do, I want them to be invisible."

"Remember that team we assembled in the Congo?"

"Oh, hell yeah. They have a U.S.-based firm here too. I'll give them a call. Gary will cover the cost."

"The houses on both sides of Jake's are rental units; I'll see if Gary can block them and place the teams there. We'll have a fortress."

~

Possum set up a FaceTime with the private security firm in Oakland, CA, explaining the situation. The CEO recommended sending in two teams that resembled vacationing families. As soon as Rick got the go-ahead from Jake to use the rental houses, the teams booked their flights to Tallahassee and would arrive within hours of each other the following day. Possum texted the plan to Rick, packed up his and Malia's gear, and called an Uber. Within thirty minutes, he stood at the back door of Jake's house. Rick let him in.

"Welcome home, y'all." Rick kissed Malia on the cheek, and she and Possum put their things away in the spare bedroom next to Rick and Jules' bedroom. Rick and Possum hopped into the Suburban, with Possum ducking down in the back seat as they headed to town.

He planned to stay with Jules and Malia, but Jules insisted that he go. She handed Malia a handgun and secured the house tighter than Fort Knox. Rick was opposed to the idea, but convincing Jules otherwise was virtually impossible. She could handle herself well, but it still gave him pause. He promised to return as quickly as possible after leading the forensics team to the body site.

After arriving in Tallahassee, Rick switched cars with the rented one and drove to the hotel where the forensic team was already checked in. He stepped into his room with Possum and knocked on the adjoining door.

"Rick Waters?" a voice asked from the other side.

"In the flesh," Rick replied.

As the door opened, they shook hands.

"We have all our forensic gear and digging tools in that black SUV parked by the exit."

"Okay, we'll ride with you, and you can park by the state park. No one will be down there right now. From there, I can lead you to the site. You have night vision, right?" Rick confirmed.

"Yeah, I have enough for everyone, including you two. We have the new ARNVGs. They are the most light-gathering, comfortable night vision goggles on the planet."

"I read about those. They are sick! I can't wait to try them," Rick replied, excitement bubbling beneath the surface.

"You're gonna want a pair. I guarantee it."

Silent anticipation hung in the air as they stealthily climbed into the black Escalade. It was Rick's first time in this Cadillac model, and though he was a Ford guy, he had to admit the sheer size of it impressed him. They drove down to the state park and disembarked. Two team members lowered an electric cart onto the sand, loaded with all the gear. The team leader handed out the night-vision goggles, and Rick was blown away as soon as he put them on. They literally turned night into day.

Leading the way to the body site, Rick and Possum maintained a discreet distance from the SUV. He secured both pairs of goggles in his backpack and called for an Uber. After informing the team leader he'd leave the goggles in the adjoining room, they took the rental car back to the Suburban, again hiding Possum in the back seat. Once parked in the garage, Rick locked it down.

"We're here, hombre."

As they strolled into the beach house, a familiar aroma filled Rick's nostrils.

"Gumbo!" he exclaimed.

"Duh, your favorite too! Chicken and sausage. We had everything we needed here. Malia made Possum's famous cornbread recipe too!"

"Oh my God! Y'all are amazing. Any issues while we were away?"

"Not exactly. Someone did drive by the house in a dark Tesla several times. The second time they came by, I snuck outside and hid behind that bush next to the driveway. I borrowed your Canon, Possum. I hope you don't mind. Anyway, snapped a photo of the license plate. It's a New Jersey plate," Jules reported.

"Reeeeaally?!" Rick exclaimed, mimicking Ace Ventura, Pet Detective.

They all laughed, and Rick examined the photo before sending it to Carson. Within fifteen minutes, he received a name tied to the plate.

Call me.

Not wasting time, Rick called Carson.

"Talk to me, buddy."

"The plate is registered to the campaign manager of Vito Profaci."

Rick couldn't help but do an Ace Ventura impersonation again.

"What do you know about him?"

"He's Italian and has no rap sheet. He has been known to associate with some seedy individuals in Jersey but has never been charged with anything. One thing that stands out, though, is that he served with Delta Force and was on the EOD. Watch yourself."

"Okay, EOD is about disarming ordinances, though, isn't it?"

"Yes, but in order to disarm, they must be knowledgeable about arming as well."

"Gotcha."

"Thanks for the quick response, Carson. The team you sent is on site. I hope it brings some revelations."

"Me too. Y'all be careful."

"We'll be fine. I have two private security teams arriving tomorrow."

"Oh, good. I was gonna suggest that. These people are hardcore."

"I hear ya. Talk to you soon," said Rick said, ending the call.

Rick joined the group, drawn in by the enticing smell of cornbread as Malia set it on the dinner table. Possum's recipe included sugar and honey, plus sour cream to keep the bread moist. Rick likened it more to corn cake rather than traditional cornbread; it was incredibly addictive.

They gathered around for dinner, trying their best to steer the conversation away from the case, but it always circled back. Rick, feeling a hint of fatigue from the ongoing situation, looked forward to a getaway after it was all resolved.

"Jules, once we are done here, we should take the motorhome down to the Everglades. There's some cool stuff down there. Maybe we can even spot a Skunk Ape," Rick suggested.

"A what?!"

"Skunk Ape. It's South Florida's name for Bigfoot."

"Really? That would be amazing! Are there places to ride the trails down there?"

"Oh, hell yeah. There's a long circular trail called Shark Valley. I've never done it, but it looks amazing online. They said you can see all sorts of birds and gators along the trail."

"We better leave Choco and Chief at home then."

"We'll see. As long as they stay in the motorhome, they'll be fine."

Post-dinner, they all convened in the theater room, where Rick pulled up a few episodes of *Finding Bigfoot*.

"Oh shit. I met that guy, Dave Shealy. He owns the Skunk Ape Research Headquarters in Ochopee, Florida. It's connected to a small RV Park that used to be called Snakes and Mosquitos."

"That sounds enticing," Jules quipped sarcastically.

"That's why they changed the name to Flamingo Campground. It sounds a little more inviting," Rick teased.

After a few episodes, they moved onto a documentary titled *Nature: Invasion of the Giant Pythons.*

"Oh, hell no!" Jules exclaimed.

Rick nearly spat out his green tea, laughing.

"They are super slow, Jules. You don't have to worry about them."

"What kind of husband wants to bring his wife to a place full of alligators, snakes, and mosquitoes?"

"The adventurist kind?" asked Rick sheepishly. "I mean, if you're scared..."

"Scared? I ain't scared. I hate snakes."

"The good news is they also have thousands of species of birds, deer, armadillos, and tons of other animals. Oh, and the fishing is out of this world."

Rick noticed Jules' eyes light up as he mentioned fishing. He had never met anyone who loved fishing more than she did.

"They have snook down there. Big ones!"

"What's a snook again?"

"It's a racing mullet."

"A what?!"

Rick launched into his joke about racing mullets.

"A fella gets dragged before the judge for catching a snook during closed season. The game warden slaps the evidence on the table: a fine specimen, scales still glistening, that telltale black pinstripe gleaming like fresh chrome.

Judge squints at it and says, "Son, this here's a snook, plain as day. You know the law—fines and community service, or worse."

The fisherman doesn't miss a beat. He leans in, points right at that stripe, and drawls, 'Beggin' Your Honor's pardon, but that ain't no snook. Nosir. That's a racin' mullet!'

The courtroom goes quiet. Judge blinks. 'A what now?'

"'Racin' mullet, Your Honor! Look at her! Built for speed, low to the water, and that pinstripe? I wasn't poachin' snook; I was trainin' my mullet for the mullet races down at the marina! This one's a thoroughbred—hit 15 knots on the line before I reeled her in. She'd smoke any snook in a straightaway!'"

Silence fell in the room, and Rick knew it was time to learn some new jokes.

CHAPTER
TEN

Rick received a call from Carson just before lunch.

"Rick, we got a hit on one of the bodies."

"One? There was more than one?"

"I'm afraid so. They found the remains of five women. Young girls, really. The one we identified through dental records was a runaway named Colby Mitchell. She was fifteen. She was last seen at a Cape May convenience store. She had called her mother from a pay phone and told her she met a guy who was gonna get her some modeling jobs. She was never seen again," said Carson.

"Cape May, New Jersey?"

"That's the one."

"Son of a bitch. I bet she was trafficked."

"That's what I was thinking," replied Carson.

"What's the plan?"

"We are going to bring a bigger team out there. I have a feeling there are more bodies."

"How are you gonna keep this discreet?"

"I won't be able to. Once the media gets ahold of this, it's gonna be a circus. I can hold off for three, maybe four days. I need to get a warrant anyway so we can bring the big team down. Since the dead girl was identified as being from Jersey, the FBI can take the lead on the case. That gives us jurisdiction."

"I understand. Hold off as long as you can. Once whoever did this finds out the FBI is on it, they will likely disappear."

"I know. Maybe I should come down there."

"I think you should. You can stay with us at Jake's place. I can pick you up in the Suburban and sneak you in through the garage. At this point, no one knows that anyone else is staying here; they think we're Jake and Cindy. The longer we can keep up this ruse, the better," said Rick.

"I get it. I'll book a flight and text you my ETA."

"Okay, Carson. See you soon."

Malia made her version of muffulettas for lunch, and Rick enjoyed the Cajun food the girls were cooking. After they ate, Rick and Possum watched as the first security team arrived at the house next door. They looked like two young couples dressed in Florida casual wear, with a beach ball and pool floats in the car. Rick knew that some of those suitcases contained weapons and surveillance gear, though. One of the men looked up at Rick and gave him a knowing nod. Rick felt safer already.

About an hour later, the second team arrived, also dressed like tourists, complete with long socks and golf shorts. While they looked harmless, Rick knew they were highly trained security professionals, likely with military backgrounds. The four women in their group looked like an average couple, but Rick noticed how they scanned the area as they approached.

Rick's phone vibrated—it was Carson's flight info.

"You wanna run with me to pick up Carson, Jules?"

"Sure. Malia, do you want me to pick up dinner, or do you have plans for tonight?"

"I think Possum and I can whip something up. I love cooking with him in the kitchen. It will be romantic."

"Okay. Sounds good. Let me grab my shoes, Rick, and I'll be ready."

They put on their Jake and Cindy outfits and headed to the garage. As they drove past Possum and Malia's rental, Rick saw a light go on and off.

"Someone's in there or Possum set timers. I'm gonna text him."

Did you set the timers in the rental house?

Yes, several. For the TV as well.

Okay, good. By the way, your Bronco has bird shit on it.

Dammit!

Rick laughed, enjoying the joke at Possum's expense.

When they arrived at the Tallahassee Airport, Carson was waiting curbside. Rick made sure no one had followed him as Carson climbed in and put his bags on the seat next to him.

"Welcome to Florida. Good flight?" asked Rick.

"Uneventful. My favorite kind."

"I hope you like Cajun food. Possum and Malia have been on a roll. I'm sure they have some cool Cajun dish planned for tonight."

"Sweet! I love Cajun food." Carson then informed Rick that the five bodies were all young girls about the same age. The DNA tests were complete, and the FBI was trying to find family members of girls who went missing around the same time in the area. It would take time.

When they approached the bridge, Carson ducked down in

his seat as Rick pulled into the driveway and into the garage, closing the door behind them.

"Okay, coast is clear. It's safe to sit up."

As they entered the house, Rick identified the delicious smell wafting through the air—it was red beans and rice.

"Is that red beans and rice I smell?" he asked.

"You've got a good nose, hombre. Now what's this?" Possum opened the oven door, flapping it a few times.

"No way! You didn't! Crawfish pie?"

"Bingo. We made two of them. I had the crawfish delivered by Instacart."

"Smart move. No one saw you, right?"

"Nope. I asked for touchless delivery. They left it at the door, and I put on one of Jake's orange caps and snatched it off the porch. Y'all are right on time. These pies just need to cool a bit, then we can serve," said Possum.

They all sat down to dinner, a feast of Cajun delights. Possum even made Tarte à la Bouillie, a custard pie that translated to burnt milk tart.

Suddenly, the entire house shook, and a glass shattered in the kitchen.

Kaboom!

A loud explosion rattled the house. Rick rushed to the front window and peeked outside.

"Possum, your rental house just exploded. Look at the flames."

"Oh no. My Bronco is on fire, too. What the fuck?!"

Rick used his burner phone to call 911. They longed to get a closer look but couldn't risk being spotted. Within minutes, sirens blared and a long line of flashing lights crossed the bridge.

"Rick, look," said Possum as he showed him his phone—he

had set up tiny surveillance cameras around the house and perimeter.

"Jules, does this look like the car that was casing this house the other night?" Rick asked.

Jules squinted at the screen.

"I can't make out the color, but it's the same make. Those Teslas are distinctive."

Rick and Possum watched helplessly as Possum's Bronco burned to the ground. By the time the fire trucks arrived, it was nearly extinguished. The gas tank never exploded, but the car was totaled.

"They knew you were staying there, Possum. They know you are part of the team. Maybe they think you were all that was left of the team? We should keep up our ruse of pretending to be Jake and Cindy. They are bound to come after us next. Now more than ever, we need to be stealthy. Carson, can you get a story to the media that Possum and Malia of Rick Waters' Private Detective Agency perished in an explosion? You don't mind playing dead, do you, Possum?"

"Ha-ha. That's what possums do best!"

"I'm gonna need two bodies. I don't know anyone in the local police department, but they need to believe that they were killed inside. Let me make a call to the bureau in Tallahassee. They can send a fixer."

Carson was on the phone for a while, but when he returned, he was smiling.

"We're all set. A homeless man and woman were found burned to death in an abandoned van. The fixer will bring their bodies in a forensic case and plant them. He will make sure

FDLE discovers the bodies. I need a swab from both of you. He will use that to identify the remains by DNA."

"You are amazing, Carson. I feel dead already," joked Possum.

Carson used a swab kit to take DNA samples from Possum and Malia. He would meet the fixer somewhere in town to pass it along.

"I can take you in the Suburban. What is his ETA?" asked Rick.

"He'll be at the rental house within two hours."

"How is he gonna hide the bodies without being caught?" asked Rick.

"I don't know. That's why they call him the fixer. The less I know, the better. He has ties to the CIA, that's all I was told. That's enough for me to keep my distance."

Rick pulled out of the garage with Carson ducked down in the back seat. He drove past the burned house, now surrounded by police officers standing around gawking. The fire trucks had left, and the fire chief's truck still sat in the driveway. He was talking to one of the cops as Rick drove by, ready to begin his investigation. An ambulance remained at the scene, likely containing the bodies the fixer had planted.

Rick parked in an alley in Apalachicola, and a man in dark clothes approached the rear passenger window. Carson handed over the DNA swabs, and the man was gone as quickly as he'd appeared.

"Holy shit. It's easy to disappear. If I ever need to fake my death, I know who to talk to," said Rick.

When they returned to the beach house, they noticed

Possum's previous rental was now surrounded by police tape. Several squad cars, the chief's truck, and some media vans were gathered outside. Rick spotted a red-headed female reporter preparing to go live with her cameraman.

Rushing back inside, they turned on the TV just in time for breaking news. The same red-headed reporter was live on the air.

"There was a terrible explosion today at the rental home behind me on St. George Island. Two bodies were found inside. Their identities have not yet been released, but we have information that they were a male and a female who had rented the house. The fire chief has not ruled out foul play but feels confident that a propane leak caused this horrible explosion. We'll have more details as they become available. For WXTL Tallahassee, I'm Maya Sargent. Back to you, Rahman."

"That's a good cover. I bet by morning, the news will announce that Possum and Malia have been identified. We need to get some info to the station somehow that they were part of our PI team and had been working a case alone here on St. George," Rick suggested.

"Good idea, Rick. I'll take care of it," said Carson.

Rick now felt confident that congressional candidate Vito Profaci was involved in the kidnapping, the explosion, and the trafficking of young girls. He had to tie it all together somehow.

"Shit, Rick. I don't know how the media got wind of the bodies found on Jake's vacant property. There's no hiding it now. What should we do?" asked Carson.

"Phew. Let me think. The news is gonna want to question Jake. There's no doubt about that. What if we agree to have him interview over the phone? I can forward his number to the burner phone he's using in Cuba. He can say he's staying to himself in the beach house as Cindy is still recovering from her kidnapping. That will play well."

"I like it. Can you coach him before the interview?"

"Yep, I'll call him now and get him ready. There will probably be media trucks outside the beach house in the morning. We'll have to be even more stealthy from now on. The good news is that no one would dare attack the house with all the media around."

"Plus, once the news is out about the five bodies, this will likely go national. It could turn into an absolute circus," Carson noted.

"That's true. They will want to see Jake's face on camera since he owns the property. Possum, can you still do that thing you do that makes someone look like they are somewhere else?"

"You mean green screen. Yes, I can. I tell you what. Let me film the living room with that fan oscillating in the background. We can upload that to the cloud, then agree to have Jake do a livestream interview on Zoom. I can route it through my laptop to a camera in Cuba. It will look like Jake is sitting right here on his laptop. I'll set it all up," said Possum.

Possum busily set up his tripod and filmed an hour of the empty great room. He created a Zoom account for Jake and synced the video to it as a backdrop. Rick called Jake to explain their plans and let him know that one of his rental houses had exploded. Jake had insurance, but he clearly felt rattled by the news.

Rick reassured him that it all seemed too real now that someone wanted them all dead. He advised Jake to do the local phone interview first, then wait for the national media to reach out and schedule a Zoom interview on Fox News or CNN.

⮑

Just as predicted, two news media vans pulled up in front of Jake's house—one from a local station and one from MSNBC. Rick knew it was about to become a carnival outside. The house phone rang in Jake's beach house, and Jules answered, adopting a more exaggerated Spanish accent.

"Hola, Mr. Richmond's residencia."

"I would like to speak to Mr. Richmond, please."

"Por que? Who may I say is calling?"

"This is Maya Sargent with WXTL, Tallahassee. I'd like to ask him some questions."

"Por supuesto. Please and may I have your number? He is muy busy," Jules replied.

After writing down the reporter's number, Jules hung up and relayed the info to Rick. He called Jake to get him ready. They planned to call the reporter back from Cuba, disguising the number to look like Jake's local phone. Possum walked Jake through the steps.

"Are you ready, Jake?"

"Yes, let's do it."

Jake dialed the reporter's number after following the procedure Possum had shown him.

"Hello, this is Maya Sargent."

"Hi, Miss Sargent. This is Jake Richmond. My housekeeper told me you called."

"Yes, Mr. Richmond. I want your response to the bodies found on your property recently. Are you aware of the situation?" asked the reporter.

"Yes. The property has been undeveloped for many years. I have no plans at this time to develop it. I'm disturbed that they found the remains of several women on the property. I will, of course, cooperate with the police on the matter. I have nothing to do with it, obviously, but I have been contacted by the FBI. As I said, I have given my full cooperation to excavate and search the property as they see fit. It's a tragic discovery."

"Do you think your daughter's recent kidnapping has anything to do with the bodies being found?"

"I have no idea. I am just a businessman. Someone was trying to obtain the property by any means, and I told the FBI as much."

"Thank you, Mr. Richmond. May I call you again if I have any further questions?"

"Sure, unless the FBI tells me not to speak any further, I don't see a problem with that. I am an open book."

Jake ended the call and switched over to Rick's line, where he listened in.

"How did I do?"

"Perfect, Jake. Perfect. We will no doubt be contacted soon by a major national news organization. Is there a particular news outlet you'd prefer to speak with?"

"No, not really. They all lie. Just make sure it's not *The View*. I hate that show."

"Don't we all," Rick chuckled.

Several more news vans rolled up outside Jake's beach house, and Rick realized it would be increasingly difficult to leave and return in disguise. He decided to wait until after the national news interview and then change their plans. Jules continued fielding calls from various outlets, and they agreed to do two interviews—one with Fox News and another with CNN.

Possum set everything up on Zoom, and Rick called Jake. He instructed him to tell the news at the end of the interview that he would be leaving the area with his daughter for safety reasons and flying to an undisclosed location. The first interview with CNN went off seamlessly, and Rick watched it live on television. The second interview with Fox News was recorded for rebroadcast on Sean Hannity's program.

As Rick and Jules disguised themselves as Jake and Cindy, wearing dark sunglasses, they exited the garage and drove off while the news cameras fought for shots of them leaving. The news reported that Jake and Cindy had departed. Rick drove to Destin and concealed the Suburban in the parking garage under their condo.

Rick fired up the Bronco, and he and Jules headed down to Destin HarborWalk to meet Johnie and check on Chief. Johnie had been bird-sitting Chief since he returned the catamaran to Destin. Olivia, Rick's office manager, had taken responsibility for watching Choco. Choco and her dog, Mattie, got along wonderfully, and Olivia loved caring for both of them when needed.

"Hey, Rick. Hi, Jules. Are y'all gonna be here a few days?" Johnie asked.

"Nah, we're heading back in the morning at sunup. We will announce to the media that we are working on the case to reach a resolution. No more disguises."

"I gotcha. Well, Chief is up in the wheelhouse chewing on some wooden bird toys."

Rick climbed up to the flybridge, and Chief dropped the piece of wood from his beak, bouncing around excitedly and flapping his wings.

"Hi, Boy, did you miss me?" Rick asked.

Chief raised the crest on his head and danced.

Rick picked up Chief and snuggled with him, then handed him down to Jules, who was just as excited to see Chief as he was. Rick called Olivia to ask if she could drop off Choco at

Rick's condo for the night, and she agreed. They all settled in for a cozy night together.

When they returned to the condo, Rick took Choco for a walk around the block. Upon returning, he ordered Thai from Thai Chiang Rai Restaurant in Santa Rosa Beach via Uber Eats —a familiar favorite from their past adventures. After a delicious meal and some shared laughs, they called it a night, needing rest for the drive back to the Forgotten Coast in the morning.

CHAPTER
ELEVEN

Steam and mist rose from the street as Rick pulled onto Highway 98 eastbound. The sky was a deep blue as they passed Destin Commons. It would've been faster to take I-10, but the drive was boring, so they decided to hug the coast. Chief sat on Jules' lap, while Choco rested his head on the console between them, enjoying the air conditioning. Rick felt apprehensive about making his presence known; facing the press would put a bigger target on his back. But at least this way, Jake and Cindy would be safe and out of the picture, allowing Rick to focus on uncovering the truth behind the crimes.

"Rick, can we drive down Front Beach Road in Panama City? It's been so long since I've seen it!" asked Jules.

"Sure, Baby. No problem."

Though Rick wasn't particularly fond of Panama City, he didn't mind the detour. It was the first place he visited in Florida right after high school. But it had changed since then.

Once the hot spot for Spring Break, the beach had been packed with kids and concerts hosted by MTV. There were two massive nightclubs, Club La Vela and Spinnaker, but Hurricane Michael in 2018 had destroyed what was once the world's largest nightclub. Now, the charm of the beach town had been replaced with towering corporate-owned timeshares and condos.

"Look, Rick! They're having a sand sculpting contest. Can we stop?"

Rick glanced at his watch. It was still early, and he was in charge of his own schedule. Though he would rather shove alcohol-soaked bamboo shoots under his fingernails than attend a sand sculpture contest, he knew it would make Jules happy, so he obliged. They pulled over, finding a paid parking spot near the beach.

He had to admit the sculptures were impressive. A smiling sun hovered over a Panama City Beach sign, complete with a tower and windmill—remarkably detailed. The standout was a pair of wizards—one holding a skull and the other casting a spell with a wand.

"Wow, that is amazing," said Rick, but Jules barely heard him because she was so focused on taking photos of all the sand sculptures. It was slow going down the beach. Every few feet, someone would approach them and want to look at Chief. Chief loved kids and would flap his wings and hop up and down on Rick's arm. Rick let several kids take their picture with him. Unfortunately, he had to leave Choco in the Bronco because dogs weren't allowed on the beach. He felt bad but made it up to him when they got back. He drove over to the bay side and threw the ball with him for several minutes. After some fun at the beach, they proceeded to Apalachicola. Upon arriving at Jake's beach house, Rick noticed several news vans parked out front—a Fox News van among them. To his astonishment, he recognized Bill Melugin, a good-looking reporter who had covered the Texas border crisis extensively.

As Rick pulled in, several reporters approached the Bronco. He rolled down the window and called Bill over.

"Bill, you want an exclusive?"

Bill nodded as Rick replied, "Meet me at the door."

Rick parked in the garage and closed the door behind them. Inside, they were greeted by Possum and Malia.

"Hey y'all. How was the trip?"

"Uneventful. Listen, you're not gonna believe this, but Bill Melugin is standing at the front door. You ready to ruffle some feathers?"

"I saw him through the window earlier. Sure, what's the angle?" Possum asked.

"We need to present a united front and let on that we're close to solving this case and will be closing in soon. Let's say we have proof that one of the candidates for Congress is involved and has ties to organized crime. We won't name names, but if we're right about what Chuck Asbury said about Vito Profaci, he'll come after us. He has no idea we have a military arsenal inside this house and that we're flanked by some top-notch personal security. Unless they shoot the place with a guided missile, they will be outgunned," replied Rick.

"I like it. I like it a lot," Possum chimed in, mimicking Lloyd from *Dumb and Dumber*.

Rick opened the door and welcomed Bill and his cameraman inside.

"Hi Bill. I'm Rick Waters. Really nice to meet you. I followed your work during the border crisis. Great job," Rick said.

"Thanks, Mr. Waters. Those were some long, hot days

down there. I'm glad that mess is over, and I hope we never have to revisit anything like it again," Bill replied.

"I agree. We deserve to be a sovereign country with closed borders and controlled immigration."

"Amen," said Bill.

"Bill, let me introduce everyone. This is Jules, my wife. She's a bounty hunter and a badass private detective. This is Possum, our critical thinker and computer whiz, and his girlfriend, Malia—an amazing cook from Hawaii and one of the best surfers I've shared a wave with. Together, we are Team Waters. But no one can know they are alive. As a matter of fact, can you announce that two members of my team were killed in an explosion? You know that house just up the street? This is Carson, an FBI agent who needs to stay off camera as well. We were hired by Jake to find his daughter, Cindy, which we did, and to determine who was behind her kidnapping and other recent crimes."

"I can do that," Bill replied.

Bill shook everyone's hands. He looked around the great room for the best place to film and decided to have the team sit on the main couch, with him doing an over-the-shoulder interview. With only one cameraman, he explained that he would ask each question twice, with the cameraman facing Bill the first time and then shooting over his shoulder the second time. It would be edited in post and most likely aired that night on either Jesse Watters's show or Laura Ingram's. Rick felt a surge of pride well up inside him. He had known those names for years, and national airtime would definitely flush out the bad guys. Bill instructed them on how to arrange themselves on the couch and went over the questions beforehand as the cameraman took measurements with his light meter and adjusted his white balance on his camera.

"You ready?" asked Bill, a consummate professional as he reviewed his notes.

Rick reminded him to mention Possum and Malia's deaths and to keep Carson out of the story. Bill nodded and began.

"I'm Bill Melugin in St. George Island, just off the coast from Apalachicola, Florida. I'm here with Rick and Jules Waters, a couple running a private detective agency from Destin, Florida. They are here today to update us on a case that has intrigued locals and caught the nation's attention. We're in the home of Jake Richmond and his daughter, Cindy, who was recently kidnapped and held for ransom but was rescued by Team Waters. Rick, what can you tell us about the case and the recent discovery of human remains on Jake's property?"

"Bill, we used a ruse to get Cindy back from the kidnappers. They're so stupid they fell for a fake CRT to transfer the land in exchange for Cindy's release," said Rick.

"CRT?" asked Bill.

"Oh, I'm sorry. A CRT is a Charitable Remainder Trust document used to donate property to an individual or corporation. I can't get into details, but they're so ignorant they gave up Cindy without having a lawyer look over the paperwork first. They are pretty dumb."

"It almost sounds like you're calling them out," said Bill.

"That's right, Bill. We know who they are, and we're right here. Come and get us; a few punks don't scare us."

"What can you tell me about the discovery of human remains on the nearby vacant property owned by Jake Richmond, and where are Jake and Cindy at the moment?"

"I can't tell you where they are, Bill. You know that. Let me just say they are in a safe, undisclosed location where no one can reach them. As for the human remains, we are working closely with the FBI," said Rick.

"I got this, Rick," Jules passionately interjected.

"Those aren't just human remains. They are young girls—innocent young girls whose lives had just begun and were taken out by pure evil."

With fire in her eyes, she leaned into the camera, her intensity palpable.

"Those girls were trafficked by a scumbag. I will personally see to it that he faces judgment or a bullet to the head if he comes after me. After being carjacked once and coming through it, I have experience dealing with lowlifes like those who took these girls out. They will pay for what they have done!" exclaimed Jules, sitting back down as her eyes welled up.

"Wow, I can tell you all mean business. I know this is more than personal for you because of the deaths of two of your team members, Possum and Malia. Do I have the names right? What leads do you have so far?" Bill asked.

"Yes, we believe the explosion that took my partners' lives was carried out by the same criminal group. We have identified one of the girls as being from New Jersey. What I'm about to tell you, Bill, will shake up Congress and shed light on a groundbreaking news event. We have confirmed that one of the Congressional candidates for the upcoming race for FL-1 District 3, vacated by Matt Gaetz who recently stepped down in his bid for Attorney General, is involved in the trafficking and murder of these girls and in Cindy's kidnapping. They are all tied together. He has ties to organized crime, and we will take him down. I won't say his name, but he knows who he is, and he will pay the ultimate price in the end."

Bill asked a few more questions and wrapped it up.

"You heard it here first, exclusively. I'm Bill Melugin from

St. George Island, Florida, with Fox News. More to come in this unbelievable unfolding saga."

As the cameraman rushed out to the news van, Bill expressed his gratitude.

"Thank you so much for the interview! Can I get your phone number? I'll text you when it airs. It's going to be a big deal. Jules, your speech was epic. This will be everywhere after it airs. You will be all over social media."

"Really? How was my hair, Rick?"

Rick laughed.

"Jules, you were a natural and looked beautiful as always. And fierce!"

Jules blushed as Rick exchanged business cards with Bill. After a handshake, Bill texted Rick to ensure he'd have his contact information. They took a few photos together, and Rick walked Bill to the door.

"I'll text you if we get any developments. If you give us proper airtime, I'll keep this exclusive."

"I don't think that's going to be a problem. Once my team gets this to New York, they'll be on it like white on rice."

Bill left, and Rick closed the door behind him.

"Well, that was fun. Let's see if it brings out the scumbags," said Rick.

"What's next?"

"Let's wait for it to air and see if they contact us. If they don't, then we were wrong. But we're not wrong," replied Rick.

Rick and Jules took Choco and Chief out to the back deck by the pool. Choco immediately jumped into the pool. Rick called Jake and got him up to speed on the Fox News interview, while Malia and Possum made lunch for the gang and worked on dinner ideas. Rick knew it might be the last day they could safely ride their bikes in the area. After a little pool time, he and

Jules took their Trek bicycles out for a ride in the neighborhood. They rode down by the beach and down toward the lighthouse. A couple was taking some grocery bags out of their car when a cat ran across the road. Jules swerved to miss it and took a spill on her bike right in front of their driveway. The man put down his grocery bag and ran out to help Jules.

"Are you okay? I saw that damn cat run out in front of you."

Jules felt embarrassed as she examined her skinned knee.

"That's gonna be quite a raspberry. Come inside. I have some peroxide, triple antibiotic, and bandages. Let's get you cleaned up."

"Thank you, sir. I'll be fine; I can do it when I get home."

"Nonsense! You don't want that to get infected. I'm Chuck Reed, and this is my wife, Linda. Y'all come in, and I'll get you both something to drink."

Knowing refusing wouldn't be an option, Jules picked up her bike, and she and Rick followed Chuck inside. Rick introduced himself and helped Linda with the groceries as she put them away. She brought out bottles of water for them as Chuck made himself a gin and tonic.

"Can I offer you a mixed drink or some wine?"

"Thank you, Linda. We both gave up alcohol, but I appreciate it," said Rick.

"Oh boy, do I have a drink for you two. Do y'all like mango?"

"Love it," Rick replied, while Jules nodded as Chuck put a large waterproof bandage on her boo-boo.

"I call it my Mango Mocktail. Let me whip a couple up for y'all," Linda said, mixing them in stemmed glasses and adding lime slices on the edge.

Rick enjoyed non-alcoholic beer occasionally but had never ordered a mocktail before, so he was pleasantly surprised.

"Wow, this is amazing! What's in this? It almost tastes like a real cocktail!"

"It's super easy, only three ingredients: two ounces of mango nectar, tonic water, and coconut water. That's it," Linda replied.

"Wow. I'm gonna start making these," Rick responded.

"Yes, please," echoed Jules.

The couple quickly warmed to Rick and Jules. Chuck was funny and good-natured, while Linda was incredibly kind and hospitable. After a few minutes, it felt as if they'd known them a lifetime.

"What brings y'all to St. George Island?" Rick asked.

"We were on a tour in our motorhome, but we got caught in a storm, and a sudden downdraft ripped off our awning. When it flipped up, it put a three-inch hole in our roof. We had to drop it off at an RV repair shop and it'll take about a week to fix, so we decided to rent a place here because Chuck had never been."

"Oh, cool. We have a motorhome too—a 44-foot Entegra Aspire. It's back in Destin, where we live. After we finish working here, we're thinking of heading down to the Everglades for a week of exploring and fishing."

"Maybe we'll see you down there! We're heading south after our motorhome is repaired," Chuck said.

"What kind of work do you do?"

"I own a private detective agency in Destin, and we're doing some work for a local guy."

"How exciting!" Linda exclaimed.

"Chuck bought way too much salmon. Would you care to join us for dinner? I'm making salmon pasta."

"I need to call my partner Possum. He may have started dinner already."

"Invite him as well! We have enough to feed an army."

"Let me call him. That's really kind of you."

Rick called Possum, who said they had marinated a brisket that could wait for another day. He asked if they could bring a dessert along.

"Linda, Possum offered to make dessert. He and his girlfriend, Malia, would love to join you for dinner with us later. Oh, and I almost forgot; my friend Carson is here too."

"The more the merrier! Dessert would be nice. How's five o'clock for a little socializing and dinner at six?"

"Perfect! I'll let him know."

Rick updated Possum and ended the call. After finishing their mocktails, they thanked Chuck and Linda and left to finish their bike ride. Jules' knee was bandaged and not too sore.

They rode for another hour, then returned to Jake's beach house to spend some time in the pool. Possum had picked up a pumpkin pie from Costco, so they decided to bring that instead of making something from scratch. They joined Rick and Jules for pool time, and Rick was reminded that those massive Costco pumpkin pies were among the best he'd ever tasted, especially at less than six dollars.

After spending time at the pool, they all showered and got ready for dinner with Chuck and Linda. Rick and Jules took the Bronco down to park a few houses away from their rental. Being cautious, they opted for a sandy path to enter through the back gate, as arranged earlier with Chuck.

Inside, Rick introduced Possum, Malia and Carson to Chuck and Linda. They settled on the back deck, where Linda mixed her famous Mango Mocktails again. Malia savored some wine, while Possum and Carson joined Chuck for a few gin and tonics. An hour of laughter and clinking glasses passed before they all sat down for dinner in the dining room.

The salmon pasta proved to be incredible, and Chuck was pleasantly surprised by the taste of the Costco pumpkin pie. He recalled the last one he'd had—too spicy and burning his throat, likely from Sam's Club rather than Costco. This one was a hit.

Once dinner ended, Chuck began to clear the dishes—an agreement between him and Linda; if she cooked, he handled cleanup. They were an endearing couple, and Rick appreciated their warmth.

Just then, Rick's phone whistled. It was a message from Bill Melugin.

Your story will air at 7:00 p.m. on Laura Ingram.

Thanks, Bill. We'll be watching.

The time on Rick's iPhone read 6:57 p.m.

"I hate to ask, but would y'all mind turning on the TV? We're about to be on Fox News," he said.

"Seriously, Fox News? How exciting!" Linda exclaimed, quickly locating the remote.

She turned on the big flat-screen TV in the living room, and they all gathered around as the segment started. It was the lead story, executed well and bound to ruffle some feathers.

"Well, we hate to eat and run, but I think y'all understand now. We can't come back here until this case is solved for your own safety," said Rick.

"I ain't scared! I've got a little baseball bat from a game," Chuck piped up, brimming with bravado.

"Plus, I have my 9-millimeter," added Linda, a note of seriousness in her voice.

"Just to be safe, let's not communicate for a while. Here's

my card. Let's try to hook up in the Everglades; we owe you a dinner," Rick suggested, handing over his business card.

"You don't owe us anything, but yes, if we can hang out in the Everglades, that would be nice. Y'all please be careful. We'll be praying for you," Linda said, concern etched on her face.

They shared hugs, feeling the weight of the moment. The gang quietly snuck out through the back gate into the darkness, ready to tackle whatever lay ahead.

CHAPTER
TWELVE

Chief once again broke out of his cage and stood on Rick's chest before 5:00 a.m. Rick cracked open one eye.

"You crazy bird. Come here."

Rick pulled Chief under the covers, and Chief tucked his head under Rick's chin and closed his eyes. Rick was always amazed by how Chief could sleep for long periods lying in bed with Rick or Jules. He would be perfectly still and keep his eyes closed the entire time. He wanted to be close to them at all times. Rick had set his phone to silent, and when he woke up a couple of hours later, he noticed several messages from Carson. He snuck out of bed, and Jules didn't move. Rick carried Chief into the kitchen, put him on the perch, and gave him some red grapes. Now that Chief was occupied. He grabbed a cup of coffee and walked into the war room to talk to Carson.

"Hey buddy, what's up? I guess I slept in a bit."

"No problem. Rick, I got a call from Quantico. They identified the four other bodies. They also found another area they're excavating now on Jake's property and believe there may be more."

"You've got to be kidding me."

"I wish I were. All five girls went missing from New Jersey and were believed to have been trafficked. These are fucking teenagers. It makes me sick!"

"It makes me sick too. Jules is gonna blow a gasket," said Rick.

"We don't have any forensic evidence tying these bodies to Vito Profaci, though. Just rumors."

"What can we do?"

"We need someone on the inside. Do you have any ideas?" Carson asked.

"Yes, I do. Let me call Gary and see if Boudreaux can take some time off from the coffee plantation in Mississippi. He used to be an enforcer with the Cajun Connection. If Profaci is involved in organized crime, he could be useful."

Rick called Gary.

"Hey, Gary. How's Cuba?"

"Magical as usual. Jake and Cindy have been helping out with the nursery and really enjoying themselves here."

"Speaking of nurseries, could you spare Boudreaux from the coffee and weed farm in Mississippi for a few days or weeks if needed?"

"I don't see why not. I spoke with Tungsten the other day, and everything is going well. You want me to call Boudreaux and get him a flight to Tallahassee?"

"If you don't mind. I need him to get close to Vito Profaci. Given his background as an enforcer, it won't be a stretch for him."

"Ha-ha, you need to stop watching *Family Guy*. Okay, I'll set it up. I'll rent him a car in Tallahassee too, and he can stay in

Apalachicola and do what he does. I'll have him report to you on his burner phone."

"Thanks, Gary. Stay safe in Cuba."

"Y'all stay safe too."

Rick refilled his coffee and joined Carson again in the war room.

"Okay, Gary's gonna set up Boudreaux to infiltrate Profaci's organization. I know he will have heard of him."

"Good. He'd better tread lightly. Vito Profaci is pure fucking evil."

"Can you imagine if he gets elected to Congress?"

"That would be a nightmare," said Carson.

"I'm gonna join the excavation team on Jake's property. Do you and Jules wanna join me?"

"I think that would be too traumatic for Jules. Why don't you take one of the four-wheelers or side-by-sides in the garage?"

"Great idea, thanks, Rick."

Carson headed out, and Rick brought a cup of coffee to the bedroom for Jules. To his surprise, he found her, Possum, and Malia out on the back deck.

"Rick, we may have a problem."

"What is it?" asked Rick.

"Last night, as we exited Chuck and Linda's place, I stuck a tiny hidden night-vision camera on their fence. Check this out."

Rick took Possum's phone and watched a video he had downloaded during the night. It showed three men dressed in black entering the backyard but never leaving.

"Rick, I called Linda, and there was no answer. I'm worried," said Jules.

"Fuck that. Let's go."

The three of them ran to the garage, and Possum asked

Malia to stay behind for her safety. They sped to Chuck and Linda's rental, pulling into the empty driveway. Chuck's Blazer was nowhere to be found.

Rick rushed to the door and rang the bell. No answer. He peeked inside and saw overturned furniture in the dining area. Pushing the thumb latch on the door handle, he found it unlocked and pushed it open, pistol drawn.

"Chuck? Linda? Are you here?"

Silence echoed. Together they cleared the house, finding no sign of them.

"Rick, come here!" yelled Jules.

"On the kitchen floor, a small baseball bat lay next to blood spatter on the wall."

Rick grabbed a paper towel and picked it up. A tiny bit of blood and some black hairs clung to it.

"Chuck must've gotten a good whack on one of them. This hair is black—his is gray and Linda's is blonde. Phew! That's a relief."

"Someone took them though, that's for sure," said Jules.

"Fuck. Why did we even come over here? We've put their lives at risk!" exclaimed Rick.

"Who could've seen us? Did someone spy on us?" asked Possum.

"I don't know, but whoever it is has eyes on us. I wonder if they know you and Malia are still alive?"

"Most likely now," said Possum. "It doesn't matter anyway. Fuck 'em!"

"I'm guessing they will be contacting us. Maybe we should get ahead of this. I'm gonna call Bill Melugin," said Rick.

Jules called 911, and Rick texted Bill, who called back swiftly. He arrived just as the police did, cordoning off the house with tape. This time, Rick had a surprise for the audience.

"Bill, as we said in the last interview, we were distraught that our partners, Possum and Malia, were killed in the nearby explosion. Well, we lied. Here they are." Possum and Malia stepped into frame.

"I want the people who did this to understand that we will take you down. You can run and hide, or you can face us head-on. We will get you. We know you took Chuck and Linda Reed. If you harm a single hair on their heads, I will personally rip your head off and shit down your neck!" exclaimed Possum.

"We'll have to bleep that, but you got your point across," said Bill.

As the taping ended, the cameraman did his thing. Rick and the team shared all they knew with the local police. Upset with himself for involving Chuck and Linda, Rick vowed to ensure their safety.

Just then, Rick's phone whistled. It was Boudreaux letting him know that his flight would arrive around five o'clock and that he'd already contacted some of Profaci's people, arranging a meeting for later that night.

Boudreaux landed at Tallahassee International Airport early, at 4:52 p.m. He made his way to Hertz Car Rental and picked up a GMC Denali. As he pulled out of the parking lot, he drove toward Apalachicola, found a dirt road, removed the license plate, and affixed a Louisiana plate he had taken from his truck. He peeled off the rental stickers and proceeded to his motel in Apalachicola.

Once checked in, he called Rick on his burner phone.

"Rick, I'm here. Meeting with Profaci's people at 9:30 p.m. at Belle's Winery and Saloon."

"Great. Listen, I'm gonna text you a photo of Chuck and Linda Reed from their Facebook page. Memorize their faces, then delete the photo. Do you have a plan to rescue them?"

"Yes, but I'll need your help. Dis will be hard. Whenever Profaci's people contact you for a trade or ransom demand, tell dem to go fuck demselves and dat you barely know de people and don't give a shit what happens to dem. You have to trust me. De best way for me to get them out of here is to make Profaci's people think dey are expendable. I know how dey think. Just trust me, cher?"

"Alright, Boudreaux. You've never let me down before. Please don't let anything happen to them. They're good people."

Boudreaux ended the call and cleaned his guns. It was a habit he had, the same one Rick had. Whenever he was nervous or apprehensive, cleaning his pistols brought him a sense of calm. As the time approached to meet Profaci's people, Boudreaux tried to return to the mental state he had when he was in the Cajun Connection. His life had changed so much since he met Rick and Jules. He was an enforcer for the Cajun Connection and had done terrible things to people over the years. Rick changed his life when he introduced him to Gary, who took him on as a partner in his coffee plantation and commercial nursery in Mississippi. He had also introduced Gary to the world of cannabis farming and had developed a hybrid called Snowflake because of how white the THC crystals were against the dark green part of the marijuana buds. It was a highly potent hybrid with 80% sativa and 20% indica. It was the rage in all the dispensaries in the Southeast. Boudreaux tightened his fist, pounded his chest, and headed out the door.

He couldn't just look the part. He had to be the part. He knew he would have to prove himself, and he would do so as soon as possible.

When he arrived, he saw three men sitting at a high-top table near the back of the winery. He knew it was them as soon as he laid eyes on them. He walked over and gave them the preset code.

"I hear de Malbec is good here."

The man in the center nodded, and Boudreaux sat down.

"So, you're looking for work?"

"Yeah. I need to make a change. I have too much heat in de Big Easy."

"What kind of skills do you have?"

"I'm de enforcer."

"You're an enforcer, huh?"

"No, I'm de enforcer."

A couple of big guys were getting loud over at the bar, and Boudreaux knew it was the perfect way to get in.

"Hey, shut de fuck up. We're trying to talk over here."

"Boudreaux wasn't a big guy. In fact, he was rather small, but looks were deceiving."

One of the big guys looked over and Boudreaux and laughed. The guy got even louder.

"I said shut de fuck up or I'll come shut you up."

"You got a problem?" asked the guy.

He was at least a foot taller than Boudreaux and looked like he was born with a steroid-infused pacifier in his mouth. The other guy was nearly as big but a little fatter and stupid looking. Boudreaux stood up and approached them.

"Listen, dis is a fine establishment, and I'd hate to wreck de bar with your faces, so let's step outside and have a chat."

The bully laughed, eager for a fight. Boudreaux led him to the alley beside the winery.

"Look, I nicely asked you to keep your voices down."

"You told us to shut the fuck up, twice," he retorted.

"Dat's my nice way to say it."

"Who the fuck do you think you are? I'm gonna fuck this guy up," the big man chuckled.

As the man telegraphed a jab, Boudreaux blocked easily, landing three left-handed jabs and a hard right. Blood dripped from the man's chin as he staggered back.

Suddenly the fatter guy rushed Boudreaux, who side-stepped him, smashing his head into the wall. After kicking him, breaking several ribs, Boudreaux turned to the still-standing thug. A flurry of punches knocked him to his knees.

"Don't get up. I'll pay your tab."

Returning inside, Boudreaux dropped a hundred-dollar bill on the bar and recommended the bartender call for an ambulance for the two thugs he had just decimated.

"Dey in de alley. One needs his ribs looked after. De other may need a new nose. Sorry for any inconvenience to your business."

Boudreaux sat back down with the Profaci crew.

"Maybe we should meet somewhere less rowdy tomorrow. We should go before de flics arrive. Dem boys is in de alley."

"Flics?" the man in the center asked.

"You know, the po-po, cops."

"Gotcha."

He handed Boudreaux a piece of paper with an address and the time 1:30 p.m., and they all left, each laying Benjamin on the table. The bartender would likely report nothing to the cops.

Step one was successful for Boudreaux; he had demonstrated he had the chops and wasn't afraid to use them. Back at his motel, he ordered a pizza, turned on the TV, and relaxed on the edge of the bed, cracking open a beer. Boudreaux was a cool cat—an ex-gangster with style.

It was 1:27 p.m. when Boudreaux arrived at the address on the piece of paper. It was an old steel warehouse, with tall weeds and a cement lot whose faded stripes marked the parking spots. He pulled his Denali on the side and went through the only door in the building. He handed over his pistol to the guard at the door and stepped inside. The same three crooked-nose guys sat at a card table under a hanging light in the center of the warehouse. There are several cars parked inside, an office on the far right wall, and another room in the back.

"We want you to meet our boss. I've already vouched for you. If he likes you, you're in. He will negotiate your terms."

Boudreaux nodded, taking a seat. Moments later, the office door swung open, and a man in a pinstriped suit strode toward the table. After one man offered him a chair, he sat directly across from Boudreaux.

"I understand you're looking for work?"

"Yep."

"They tell me you can take care of business."

"Dey don't lie."

"What's your expertise?"

"Enforcement and collections."

Vito sat quietly and looked at Boudreaux. He pulled out a piece of paper and a pen and slid them across the table. Boudreaux unfolded the paper, picked up the pen, scratched out the number, and wrote a larger one beneath it. He slid it back to Vito. Vito picked it up, raised an eyebrow, and nodded as if he were impressed with Boudreaux's cockiness.

"If I accept this number, what else can you do?"

"I can make anyone or anything disappear. No body, no crime."

Vito nodded, standing up. Boudreaux was in. No need for code anymore; they were now a part of the same team. One of the men handed Boudreaux an envelope filled with cash and a burner phone.

"We'll be in touch."

Boudreaux left, returning to his motel to check for bugs. After showering to cover his phone call, he dialed Rick on his old burner phone.

"Rick, I'm in. Waiting for my first assignment."

"Try not to break too many laws, Boudreaux. We need you at the coffee farm."

"I'll do my best, boss. I'll keep you posted."

"Sounds good. Be careful."

They ended the call, and Boudreaux was hungry. He hadn't eaten anything, so he headed into town and stopped at Owl Café to grab a bite and wait for his call.

Jules saw a car stop by the mailbox and put something inside it. Once it was out of sight, she ran outside to collect it. It was a large manila envelope. She took it inside, stepped into the war room, and gave Rick the envelope. Inside was a photo of Chuck and Linda, seated in chairs, with today's newspaper sitting across Chuck's chest on his lap. They looked scared, but Rick couldn't see any black eyes or busted lips, so he was happy about that. On the back of the photo was phone number.

Rick picked up his burner phone and called it. A man picked up on the other end.

"Deed to the property or they both die."

Rick took a deep breath and struggled to say it, but it came out.

"Nice try, asshole. I don't really know these people. Fucking kill them for all I care," and then he hung up.

He ran his fingers through his hair. That was so hard for him to say. He prayed that Boudreaux was right and that Rick hadn't just signed Chuck and Linda's death sentence. His phone rang again—it was the same number.

"We aren't joking. You want us to kill them?"

"Look, motherfucker. I don't care if you kill them and put their bodies in a wood chipper. I just met them and they mean nothing to me. Now fuck off!"

Rick hung up again, sweat trickling down his forehead, hands shaking. He knew he could never forgive himself if anything happened to Chuck and Linda. Turning off the burner phone, he tried to relax. Jules handed him a Heineken 0.0 and a Xanax. Reluctantly, he took them, knowing they'd help.

Within minutes, his nerves settled, but worry gnawed at him. He had acted as Boudreaux instructed; now all he could do was pray.

CHAPTER
THIRTEEN

B oudreaux's burner phone pinged at 6:17 p.m. It was a
text:

Come to warehouse.

Boudreaux hopped into his Denali and drove to the warehouse. Upon arrival, one of the men from the wine bar handed him the keys to Chuck's Blazer.

"Make it all go away. Here's a bonus." The man tossed him a paper sack.

Boudreaux tucked it under his arm and headed toward the rear of the warehouse. He climbed into Chuck's Blazer, his heart racing as he noticed the blanket covering two unmoving forms.

Son of a bitch!

He prayed they had been drugged, not killed, but he didn't dare reveal his anxiety. Exiting the parking lot onto Highway 98, he headed west. When he approached Port St. Joe, he turned right onto FM 71, finding a secluded road leading to

Lake Wimico. He parked near the lake; it was remote enough that cell reception was surprisingly strong.

Taking a deep breath, he opened the back of the Blazer and ripped off the blanket. Chuck's chest was rising and falling—thankfully, they were alive but unconscious. He always kept a bottle of AHHH!!!, the potent smelling salts promoted by Joe Rogan, in his backpack for workouts. He cracked open the bottle and held it under Chuck's nose.

Chuck jerked awake, startled but still disoriented. His mouth was taped shut, so Boudreaux quickly reassured him.

"Relax, I'm a friend of Rick's. I'm here to wake Linda now."

Walking around, he opened the back door on the other side and did the same with Linda. She bolted awake, eyes wide with fear.

"Remain calm. I'm a friend of Rick's and I'm here to save you. You have to trust me."

After some coaxing, they both nodded.

"I'm gonna remove the tape. This might hurt a little."

Boudreaux counted, "On three. One, two…" He ripped the tape off Chuck's mouth.

"Son of a bitch! What happened to three?!"

"It's easier if you aren't expecting it."

He moved back to Linda's side, repeating the process.

"Ready? One…" He ripped the tape off.

"Son of a beebum! You didn't even say two. That didn't hurt as much as when I get my upper lip waxed, though."

"Good. Glad you're okay."

Boudreaux took out his pocketknife, preparing to cut the zip ties binding them.

"Okay, you have to trust me. I'm gonna help you both out of the Blazer, and I'm gonna shoot you."

"You're gonna what?"

"I'll use blanks. But I need you both to be the best actors you can be. Rick said you met Possum, right?"

"Yeah, we met him. He's lovely," said Linda.

"He's a computer guru. After I film you getting shot with my phone, I'll forward it to him. He can use his CGI tricks to make it look like you have bullet holes and lots of blood. Got it?"

"Are you sure it will work?" Chuck asked.

"Yes, he's amazing. Now I need you to react. I'm gonna put the tape back on your mouths. It's not that sticky now, so it won't hurt. We'll take it off again. I'm gonna shoot Chuck first in the chest, and then in the head. Oh, Chuck, you need to jerk when you hear the gun go off. You know, like you've been hit. Linda, I need you to panic and start trying to escape. Then I'm gonna shoot you in the back and in the back of the head. Got it?"

"This is exciting," said Linda.

"You are one cool, calm, and collected lady, I must say."

"It's all very James Bondish," replied Linda.

"Okay, are y'all ready to be shot?"

"Fire away!" exclaimed Linda.

Boudreaux held his gun with one hand and his iPhone with the other.

"Now remember, Chuck. Once I shoot you and you jerk, don't move after that."

"Got it."

Boudreaux began filming.

"See you in hell." He fired at Chuck's chest, then at his head. Chuck's timing was perfect as he fell back, laying motionless. Linda squirmed, trying to get away, so Boudreaux fired at her back and then the back of her head. Her head slumped over, and she went still.

"Bravo, y'all are naturals!" he exclaimed.

Using his pocketknife, he cut the zip ties and helped Chuck and Linda to their feet. Then, he called Rick.

"Hey Rick, I have someone who wants to talk to you." He held the phone to Linda's ear.

"Rick, oh my God, it was so cool. Your friend. What's your name?"

"Boudreaux."

"Boudreaux fake shot us to death! It was like we were in a James Bond movie. Here, talk to Chuck."

She handed the phone to Chuck.

"Hey, Rick. Thanks for saving our asses." Rick breathed a sigh of relief, crossing himself.

"You're welcome. Boudreaux is the man. Now listen. Oh, wait, can I talk to Boudreaux?"

"Rick, I'm just gonna put you on speaker. We're in the middle of nowhere," said Boudreaux.

"What do they want for proof of death? Please tell me not their heads," Rick asked anxiously.

"No, they didn't specify. I filmed it with my iPhone. I'm gonna email it to Possum. Can you ask him to do that CGI thing he does to make it look bloody? That will be fine. They trust me."

"You got it. Send it as soon as we hang up, and I'll have him fire up his MacBook."

"Will do," replied Boudreaux.

"Chuck and Linda, listen carefully. When you leave, head to the Holiday Inn Resort Panama City Beach. Park on the second-floor underground parking. Stay there until your motorhome is ready, then head down to the Everglades. I'll meet y'all there once we wrap this case."

"Okay, Rick. Do we use our real names at the resort?"

"Yeah, that's fine. They won't be looking for you there. Just lay low. Enjoy the pool and the beach. I'm sorry I got you involved."

"Don't be. It was fun. Call me Bond, Linda Bond."

Chuck drove them back to Highway 98, thanking Boudreaux once more before getting out. He started walking back toward Apalachicola and caught a ride with a trucker heading east. Once at his motel, he waited for Possum to send him the edited video, then called for a ride back to the warehouse.

When he arrived, he showed the video to the men waiting.

"Where's the SUV?" one of the men asked.

"Bottom of a lake."

"What lake?"

"It's best I don't tell you. Plausible deniability, you know?"

"Good job. We'll be in touch."

Boudreaux left, returning to his motel. He cracked open a beer and munched on leftover cold pizza. *Fake-murdering two people today was oddly fun;* he thought, *and I didn't even feel any remorse.*

The next morning, Rick brewed a cup of coffee while Possum scrambled eggs. Carson was still out, having arrived home around 5:15 a.m. after spending hours at a new dig site on Jake's property. He finally emerged from his room a little after ten, stumbling tiredly toward the pool.

"Morning, sleepyhead. I have some news for you."

"So do I. You go first."

"Chuck and Linda are safe and free now. It's a big story, but with Boudreaux on the inside, we've got a mole."

"That's great news! Mine's a little grim—actually, a lot grimmer. They found eight more bodies last night. They think one was buried there less than a month ago."

"Oh my God, eight more? All women?"

"No, all young girls. I'm disgusted. We're trying to get DNA matches now."

"I can't believe this. It's a tragedy," said Rick.

"It's starting to feel like a Ted Bundy rerun," Carson replied.

"Can you determine the cause of death for any of them?"

"Yes. Two were definitely ligature strangulation—same as the other five girls, we think. Some were too decomposed to tell."

"You think the same person did all these, or are there more than one killer working together?"

"It's impossible to say at the moment. It's obviously the same crime ring, but they could've used more than one murderer."

Suddenly, bullets ripped through the fence as automatic weapons fired onto the deck area.

"Duck!"

Everyone dropped to avoid the hail of gunfire. Rick dashed inside to grab his pistols, charging out again, guns blazing. While he fired, the rest of the gang rushed inside. The gunfire stopped as quickly as it had begun, and Rick ran to the fence to see the getaway car—but there was nothing in sight.

Then he heard a whirring sound overhead. He looked up and spotted a drone descending swiftly. Possum rushed out with his shotgun.

"Possum, look!" yelled Rick, pointing at the sky.

Possum was the best duck hunter Rick knew, and his sharp aim led the drone to its fate with a single shot. It crashed onto the roof of the beach house.

Rick sprinted upstairs, opened a second-story window, climbed out, and retrieved the drone. He brought it back down, where Possum examined it using Google Image Search.

"It's an AR-1 drone with an attached M-27 military assault rifle that shoots 5.56mm rounds. You know what that means, right?" asked Possum.

"No freaking clue."

"It means this came from the military. It's a prototype. Only someone in the military or with military ties could access it."

"Okay, I'm still lost. The military is shooting at us?"

"No, goofball. Someone with military connections. Like a congressman or someone running for Congress."

"What do we do with it? Destroy it?"

"Fuck no! I'm gonna repair it, hack into it, and design a navigation app for my iPhone," said Possum, excitement bubbling in his voice.

"That's highly illegal, isn't it?"

"So is shooting at civilians, last time I checked!"

"True dat. Is everyone okay? Did anyone get hit?"

They all shook their heads, no. The drone wasn't accurate; a few bullets hit the fence but none reached the backyard.

Possum took his newly acquired toy inside and started taking it apart. He found a serial number and, after hours of digging around for information, discovered it was being tested at Tyndall Air Force Base in Panama City. As he suspected, it was truly a prototype.

Torn between returning it and keeping it, he recalled the saying about possession and Rick's sport fisher named Nine-Tenths: *Possession is nine-tenths of the law.*

The only damage to the drone was two of the props and the landing gear. Possum was stoked and knew he could repair it. He pulled out the CPU and messed with it. It was complex, but once he removed the chip and did some research, he was certain that with enough effort he could tweak his DJI Mini 4 Pro controller and make it fly. Carson had never even seen one like it, and he still worked with the FBI under contract. The fact that it could be so small and carry such a large, heavy weapon gave Possum an idea. He decided to see if he could mount a BILLY GOAT-15 to it instead of the heavy M-27. It would have more range and more flight time. The BILLY GOAT weighed only 4.2 pounds, while the M-27 more than doubled its weight at 9.6 pounds. Possum's BILLY GOAT was in Rick's battle box. Plus, he didn't own an M-27. Now he did.

"I guess you're gonna be wearing your inventor's hat for a while, huh?" asked Rick.

Possum just shook his head up and down like a little kid.

"Okay, I'll leave you to it."

Rick returned to the deck with Jules, Malia, and Carson. Carson had just been on the phone with the lab in Quantico and learned that the most recently buried body had been identified through jewelry and clothing. Preliminary identification indicated she was taken from a mall in New Jersey on her fourteenth birthday. Videos of her had surfaced pre-death, showing her working the streets of Miami. She had reached out to her mother, who called the Miami PD to rescue her, but she vanished after that call. The tragedy weighed heavily on everyone's hearts.

Rick called Boudreaux to check for updates.

"Hey, Bud. Anything new?"

"Not yet, but I think I'll be moved to collections soon. In addition to being a scumbag sex trafficker, I think Vito is also a loan shark. His rates are outrageous. He invests in legit businesses and charges interest like payday loan companies would envy. I'm trying to get a look at the books. Maybe tomorrow.

They're having a meeting at some fancy Italian restaurant in Panama City, and if I'm not part of it, that will give me a window. I might need some backup. You still have that taser gun? Wanna go do some shooting tomorrow?"

"Hell to the yeah! Count me in."

"Okay, I'll text you a meet-up location if it happens."

"Sounds good. Thanks, Boudreaux."

As Possum immersed himself in his drone project, Rick, Malia, and Jules made dinner. He called it a night around midnight, while Possum hadn't left his workspace except for bathroom breaks.

At around 4:30 a.m., Boudreaux finally went to bed. For a change, Rick was up before him. Taking full advantage of the quiet, he prepared Possum's famous biscuits and gravy, along with a generous side of bacon, placing a fan in front of the sizzling pan to spread the delicious aroma toward the slumbering tech wizard.

It worked; shortly after Rick started cooking the bacon, Possum staggered into the kitchen, still groggy but drawn by the heavenly scent. He poured himself a coffee and returned to work on his drone.

"Hey, hombre, you got that thing flying yet?" Rick asked.

"Almost. I need a special chip. I think I can get it from Amazon, but I realized too late, so I'll grab some coffee and get my readers so I can order it."

"Alright, well, don't forget to breathe today. Holler at me when you want breakfast," Rick said.

The aroma of bacon wafted throughout the house, waking everyone—Chief waddled across the kitchen floor and hopped onto the counter.

"Here ya go, boy. Have a small piece."

Rick handed Chief a piece of bacon, and the bird looked

adorable holding it with his foot and nibbling happily. Choco, looking jealous, got a piece too. Then Jules shot Rick puppy dog eyes and smiled, pouting her bottom lip.

"Come here, baby."

Rick fed Juels a piece of bacon, too. He then had everyone make a plate, and they all sat on the outside porch and had breakfast. As Rick was cleaning up, there was a knock on the door. Jules ran and answered it. She peeked through the window in the door, and it was the mailman.

"Hi, I need a signature for this one."

Jules signed for it. He handed her an envelope and the rest of the mail. The envelope was from Lloyds of London. She set it on the kitchen counter and helped Rick finish cleaning the breakfast dishes and pans.

Rick took the mail and put it in the box with the rest of the accumulating mail. The stack had grown quite large, so he thought he should call Jake to see whether he wanted Rick to FedEx the box to him or go through it to see if there was anything he needed Rick to open, like a past-due bill or something.

"Good morning, Jake. Are you enjoying Cuba?"

"Yes. It's been nice just to relax in the nursery and not focus on real life for a while."

"How is Cindy?"

"She's doing great. She's an emotionally strong person. Always has been. That's why I wasn't too worried that she would have any PTSD, whatever new-fangled mental name they're using these days, would be an issue after her kidnapping."

"That's good to hear. Keep an eye on her. Those things can creep in if not addressed. I have a big pile of mail for you. Do you want me to box it up and FedEx it to Cuba, or should I open it and scan it for you?"

"No! Don't open my mail!" Jake said quickly.

"Okay, not an issue. I'm just trying to help."

"Oh, I know, Rick, and I appreciate it. I'll deal with it later. I am expecting a form from Lloyd's of London. Can you see if that came? It's important."

"Hang on."

Rick sorted through the mail, spotting the envelope Jules had just signed for.

"It's here. What do you want me to do with it?"

Silence enveloped the phone as Jake pondered.

"Can you just send that one?"

"I suppose so. I can run to FedEx and get it out today."

"Thanks, Rick. Any idea how much longer you'll be on the case? We're eager to restart the brewpub project."

"I'm not sure. Soon, I hope. We have some leads."

"What kind of leads?" Jake asked.

"There may be a link to organized crime in New Jersey and a congressional candidate."

"It's a long story anyway. We've got it covered."

"You're doing a fine job. Keep it up."

"Will do, Jake. Y'all hang in there, and I'll get this envelope sent to you by tomorrow, most likely."

Rick ended the call with Jake, took the envelope, and grabbed his keys.

"Jules, I need to run to the FedEx office. Want to come?"

"Nah, go ahead. Malia and I are about to do a video workout in the gym. Gotta work off some of that bacon."

"Okay, baby. Be back soon." Rick tucked his pistol behind his back and hopped into his Bronco in the garage. He laid the letter on the seat and sipped his coffee as he drove. He kept glancing at the letter, and his curiosity was getting the best of him. He noticed the edge was peeling up, so he held it over the top of his hot coffee thermos and let the steam from the cup creep into the glue holding the letter closed. He drove with one hand while holding the letter in place. It began to loosen, so he pulled over and peeled it open slowly, making sure not to tear it. It finally opened all the way. Inside was a letter and a check for five million dollars.

Five million?! What the fuck?

Made out to Jake Richmond, the check had a code for the coverage. Rick snapped a photo of the cover letter before putting everything back inside. He searched for the code online but only found a business page, so he forwarded the info to Possum's email and continued to FedEx. The payout code was *RW*, classified under Business Risk Assessment. Likely a business liability thing, he felt guilty for snooping.

Resealing the letter with some Elmer's stick glue he picked up at Dollar General, he dropped it off at FedEx. On his way back, he spotted some Beggin' Strips and picked up a bag for Choco.

As he drove, his phone pinged with a text from Boudreaux.

Urgent, meet me at the Google Pin I'm dropping.

Rick's phone whistled again; when he entered the pin, Google Maps opened, directing him toward a two-track dirt road just off Highway 98. Following the winding side road, he arrived at a clearing, but no one was there.

Where are you?

En route, ten minutes.

Turning off his Bronco, he rolled down the windows and waited. Almost ten minutes later, a Denali pulled up—it was Boudreaux.

"What's going on?"

"When I heard de meeting was at an Italian restaurant, I thought it was dinner time. I was wrong. They just left, and I received a message to be on standby. When I asked if I should attend, they laughed, saying it didn't concern me. It was a dig, implying I was too new."

"Do you have your tranquilizer gun?"

"Yeah, I'm loaded for bear. It's all in my case in the back of the Bronco. I loaded it yesterday when you told me about the mission."

"Okay, der's one security guy outside and one inside. We need to take 'em both out without alerting each other."

"What about security cameras?" Rick asked.

"They have frequent power outages at de warehouse. It's old and only has a hundred-amp service. Sometimes it overloads, and the breaker flips. I'll trip it when you take your first shot. That'll draw out the second guard."

"How fast-acting is the tranquilizer dart?"

"Instantly. Possum created the serum himself. It has propofol and GHB along with some other stuff. It knocks someone out instantly, and they won't even remember being hit by the dart. They'll wake up thinking they dozed off. It lasts about fifteen minutes," Rick explained.

"Perfect, we should be out in less dan ten minutes."

Rick silently followed Boudreaux through the woods, careful not to break any twigs. As they reached the warehouse parking lot, Rick spotted the security guard sitting on a chair, smoking a cigarette.

Boudreaux moved closer to the breaker box, positioned on the edge of the property. He waved to Rick, who placed his air rifle against a tree and peered through the scope. Taking a deep breath, he carefully aimed and squeezed the trigger.

Pew!

The dart struck the guard on the left side of his neck. When he reached up to swat it away, assuming it was a bug, he slumped over, falling off his chair. Rick quickly reloaded another dart into his gun and waited.

Boudreaux flipped the breaker, shutting off all the power to the building. The second guard emerged from a side door, heading for the breaker box. Rick aimed and struck him in the neck as well. He collapsed instantly.

They rushed over, carrying the first guard to the door. Rick propped him back in his chair, noticing a wasp next to the door. An idea sparked in his mind.

Donning bright LED headlamps, they carried guard number two back inside, laying him in his chair with his head and arms on the desk, as if he were taking a nap. They quickly began sorting through the files in the office.

Keeping one eye on the guard and the other on his watch, they worked quickly.

"Ten minutes is coming up soon."

"He might wake up. He's a big guy," Boudreaux warned.

"Do you have any more darts?" Rick asked.

"Yes. Great idea."

As the guard began to stir, Rick swiftly jabbed a dart into his neck. Then he hurried over to the other guard, who was still slumped, and administered another dart.

They now had an extra ten minutes to gather more evidence. They managed to photograph all the files in the office and Rick flipped through a Rolodex, snapping photos of all the contacts, barely even registering the names.

At the nineteen-minute mark, they darted out of the building. Rick grabbed a broom next to the door and knocked down the wasp nest before racing back into the woods with

Boudreaux close behind. Once they reached safety, they flipped the breaker back on, making their way to their SUVs.

Gasping for breath, they high-fived each other.

"I'll forward all de photos I took to Possum's email. Let me know what you find," said Boudreaux.

"Will do. Great job, buddy. Talk to you soon."

Rick hopped back into his Bronco and headed to the beach house, his mind racing with thoughts of the successfully executed operation and the information they'd gathered.

CHAPTER
FOURTEEN

Rick was surprised to find Possum not working on the drone when he arrived at the beach house.

"Did you give up, hombre?" he asked.

"No, I ordered a part from Amazon. Can't do any more until it arrives."

"Gotcha. Well, that's good because I have a job for you. I need you to go through all these photos and see if there's any evidence we can use to take down Profaci."

"You'll also get more from Boudreaux in your inbox. I know it's a hassle, but you're the best at this."

"No big deal. I created a program that will match any name, cross-reference it, and create a database of information. I'll just need to convert all the photos to PDFs first. That will take the longest, but once it's done, it can all be processed as text and easily referenced."

"I knew you were the right man for the job. Just give me a heads-up if anything jumps out at you."

"Will do," said Possum.

Rick found Jules on the treadmill, doing a cool-down walk.

"Damn, girl! How long did you work out? I've been gone over an hour."

"It was a forty-five-minute video, then I decided to run on the treadmill for another twenty minutes. I'm almost done."

"You must be pooped."

"Nope. I feel invigorated, actually."

"Well, good for you. Meet me at the pool shortly?"

"You betcha."

Rick walked out to the deck with a bag of Beggin' Strips for Choco. Scanning the ingredients, he saw Red 40, Yellow 5, and Yellow 6. Checking the Purina website, he learned they had removed those ingredients from newer versions. Seeing the bag was nearing its expiration date, he tossed it and gave Choco some real bacon instead. *Real food is healthier than processed junk.*

After changing into his shorts, Rick cannonballed into the pool. Carson was on the phone, but he walked over and sat down, dipping his legs into the water. He laid his phone down and shook his head.

"What's up?" Rick asked.

"They've identified all the bodies. Every single one was an underage girl. The oldest was seventeen, and all went missing from the same area in New Jersey."

"Is this the work of a serial killer?"

"Technically, yes. A serial killer has to have killed three or more people. But we may be dealing with a serial killing organization, like the cartels in Mexico, responsible for the deaths of thousands of girls, dealers, or anyone who crosses them."

"It's a fucked-up world," Rick sighed.

"Yes, it is. I need a drink. This shit is getting to me."

"This early?"

"As they say, 'It's nine a.m. somewhere,'" Carson laughed.

He returned with a huge Bloody Mary.

"That looks delicious. I think I'll make one of Linda's famous Mango Mocktails."

Rick whipped one up for himself and one for Jules. Malia soon joined them, making a Bloody Mary instead. They all lounged by the pool, while poor Possum toiled away in the war room. Rick knew he was in his element and wouldn't care about missing pool time.

After a few hours, Rick checked on the brisket smoking since the night before. The amazing aroma filled the air. Time to pull it out and let it rest for four hours. After preheating the oven to 140 degrees, he set the brisket inside and set the timer.

Since Possum had started the brisket, it was a joint effort—the gang often worked well together. Jules would prepare her always-loved mustard potato salad, and Malia pre-made Hawaiian yeast rolls so heavenly they could be a meal on their own.

They enjoyed the pool until mid-afternoon, when Rick began to feel like a prune. He, Jules, and Carson ventured into town for lattes or cappuccinos at Apalachicola Chocolate & Coffee Company, giving Malia and Possum some privacy. Rick knew only Malia could get Possum to take a break, and she deserved some time with him.

Kirk Lynch and his wife, Faith, were working as usual. Jules waved, flashing a Dawn McKenna book, and Kirk gave a thumbs-up.

"Carson, you have to try one of those maple apple fritters. They should be illegal," Rick urged.

"Will do."

Rick ordered a chocolate mocha latte, Jules opted for a matcha tea latte, and they also got two cannoli. Carson grabbed a brewed coffee and a fritter. The coffee and lattes overshadowed anything they'd ever gotten from Starbucks.

Rick loved supporting mom-and-pop businesses whenever possible and did his best to shop local. Sure, he occasionally stopped at Starbucks, but he preferred little places wherever he went.

As they exited, Rick's phone pinged. It was a text from Possum:

I think I found something. I'll show you when y'all get back. Can you pick me up a six-pack of good IPA and a bottle of red wine for Malia?

You got it, buddy.

After leaving the coffee shop, Rick walked over to Oyster City Brewing to grab a six-pack of Apalach IPA. Carson picked up a six-pack of Hooter Brown while Jules found a nice bottle of red wine at a nearby gift shop. They headed back to the beach house, where they found Possum on the back deck smoking a cigar and Malia lounging on a chair.

"Honey, we're home," Rick called to Possum.

Possum quickly extinguished his cigar, dragging Rick and Carson to the war room. Jules put the beer in the fridge and joined Malia on the deck.

"Check this out! You see this payment to J. Riggs for twenty-five thousand dollars?"

"Yeah, so?"

"Well, my antenna went off. I did some research. Guess who's a bigwig at Tyndall Air Force Base?"

"Who?" asked Rick.

"Chief Master Sergeant Jason W. Riggs. Now look here; it's another one. This time it says JW Riggs. Coincidence? I think not."

"What does that mean?"

"Drone, duh!" exclaimed Possum.

"Oh, so they paid JW Riggs to get their hands on that drone."

"More than one, obviously."

"But here's the best part. The check was mailed, so that's mail fraud. We can charge Vito Profaci with mail fraud and maybe use RICO," said Possum.

"You're damn right we can use RICO. I'll start working on a search warrant. That evidence is solid, but we won't be able to use it in court. How do I explain how we got it?" asked Carson.

"You make a valid point, Carson," Rick acknowledged. "Just send in your boys to obtain that evidence legally."

Rick called Chuck Asbury to see if he had insights into any connections between Profaci and the Master Sergeant at Tyndall.

"Hi Chuck. It's Rick Waters."

"Hey, Rick. What can I do for you?"

"Are you familiar with Jason W. Riggs at Tyndall Air Force Base?"

"Yes, I am. He's attended several fundraisers and events I've been to. Why?"

"Do you know if he's cozy with Vito Profaci?"

"I don't know about an endorsement, but it's funny you mention that. We're always seeking campaign cash, and one of my staff members reached out to him for his endorsement. He said he was undecided. One of my staffers attended one of Profaci's fundraisers, and Riggs was there. Apparently, they were sitting next to each other, whispering now and then. I assumed he was planning to endorse Profaci. All candidates send their staff to monitor each other's fundraisers; it's legal, of course."

Carson disappeared to round up the troops and secure the

search warrant. The case had grown much bigger than Rick anticipated. What began as a simple kidnapping and extortion case now involved mail fraud, RICO, serial killers, and sex trafficking.

All Rick could envision was casting a rod in the Everglades with a *Heddon Chug'N Spook Popper* on the water surface, watching as a snook blasted it from beneath. But he needed to focus on closing this case before any fishing expeditions. A boy could dream, though.

He decided to call Boudreaux for any new developments.

"Hey, buddy."

"Are you psychic?" Boudreaux replied, surprised.

"No, but I have ESPN," Rick joked.

"I was just about to call you. I got word from de top made dog; they want me to make some collections."

"As in protection money?"

"Yes. As in, get de money or inflict de pain. I ain't all about dat anymore."

"I understand entirely. Two questions: Are you going alone? And do you have an amount? I have an idea."

"Yes, I'm going alone, and I have to collect 2,500 from another."

"Okay, I'll go with you. I'll bring that amount of money, and we can speak to the people. I'll let them know I'm working with the FBI—that this will all be over soon and that they should make sure to say Boudreaux took my money, that I'll never cross him. That way, if any other wise guys come around, they'll have their story straight."

"Dat's a great idea, Rick. I really didn't wanna break anyone's legs today. Can you meet me by five?"

"Yeah, no problem. I have that much cash in my go-bag."

Rick kept a go-bag with him wherever he went. Inside,

there were two fake passports for him and Jules and 10,000, he was ready for any situation.

He opened his bag, putting 2,500 in another. He explained to Jules what he was about to do, and she dropped him off in town. A few minutes later, Boudreaux arrived and picked him up.

"How'd the doctored fake murder video go over with your boss?" asked Rick.

"I think I'm about to be a made man. Ha-ha, not really. That takes years. But I do think they trust me completely now, and I am their permanent enforcer. That's a catch-22 because now they'll ask me to do things I will never do again. Like today," Boudreaux reflected.

"I get it, but we just need a little more time. In a day or two, the FBI will swoop in, and you can head back to Mississippi. Carson is already working on the search warrants. This case is growing fast."

They drove over to Eastpoint and stopped at Eastpoint Beer Company.

"They are pressuring a brewery?"

"Yeah. This one and Oyster City. I thought we'd handle this one first, then head back since they're too busy over there," said Boudreaux.

"That's odd. These aren't huge businesses. They're really asking for a lot of protection money," said Rick.

"I know, and apparently, it's doubled each time. They can't sustain these levels; they'll end up folding."

Rick stepped inside, sat down, and took in the atmosphere. It had that welcoming mom-and-pop vibe. A waitress approached, and he asked if they had a non-alcoholic beer on draft. She mentioned they were developing one but for now had Heineken 0.0 in bottles. Rick ordered one and requested to speak to the owner.

After a few minutes, Josh Parker, the owner, approached.

"Hi, I'm Josh Parker. How can I help you?"

Rick extended his hand in greeting.

"Hi, I'm Rick Waters. Can we speak somewhere a little more private? It's about the money you've been paying an unsavory character weekly, and I can help stop it."

Josh's face shifted, showing shock and concern.

"Sure, follow me. We can talk in the back."

Josh led him to the brewing area, polished stainless-steel tanks gleaming under the lights, before steering him to his office.

"It seems a little ominous. What's going on?" Josh asked.

"Listen, I know you're getting shaken down for protection money, and I know who's doing it. The collector is sitting outside in his SUV, working undercover within the organization. So what I'm about to tell you must remain confidential; his life depends on it. Do you understand?"

"Look, I'm from New York. This ain't my first rodeo. I know what the mob is capable of. This community took me in, and I am now giving back. During COVID, we had to shut down, and they supported me. I'll do anything to keep this place a go-to spot for fun, laughter, and smiles."

Rick nodded, impressed. "That's why I'm here. They want $2500 this week. I'm gonna pay it myself so you can keep my inside guy safe. The FBI is working on search warrants, which I know for a fact will be followed by arrest warrants. This will all be over soon. I just need you to play along."

A grin spread across Josh's face.

"1,200 last week. It keeps doubling in price. You have my

full support," said Josh, standing to shake Rick's hand with enthusiasm.

"Remember, if anyone asks, Boudreaux made you pay. Keep that name in mind, and say he's a scary dude."

"Boudreaux. Got it!"

Rick returned to the brewery, finished his Heineken 0.0, and rejoined Boudreaux in the Denali.

"How'd it go?" Boudreaux asked, curious.

"You're golden. He agreed to work with us. Josh is a good guy. You need to remember his name: Josh Parker."

Boudreaux jotted down Josh's name in his notes app before driving back over the bridge to Apalachicola. They parked a block away from Oyster City Brewing Company, which was still busy. A few seats were available on the porch.

Rick donned his hoodie, and they took a couple of seats. Boudreaux went inside to grab Rick a local non-alcoholic beer and a Hooter Brown for himself. They sipped their drinks and conversed while the bartender informed Boudreaux the manager would arrive within half an hour.

Rick looked up the manager on his phone to recognize her when she arrived. The brewery was owned by a conglomerate called Made By The Water, LLC, but the manager wasn't a he; it was a she—Meghan Davis.

"There she is. I'm gonna give her a few minutes to get situated, then I'll approach her," said Rick.

They continued sipping their drinks, and after Meghan had settled into her routine, Rick walked over to her.

"Meghan Davis?"

"Yes?"

"Hi, I'm Rick Waters. Can I have a word with you in private? It's about the money you've been paying an unsavory character weekly, and I can make it stop." He gestured to his nose, a

signal indicating mafia involvement. She understood immediately.

Meghan, a slender, attractive brunette with a friendly
demeanor, led Rick to her office without hesitation.

"Have a seat, Mr. Waters," she said, closing the door
behind him.

"Call me Rick."

Rick repeated the same speech he had given Josh at Eastpoint Brewing Company. She was on board as well. The big
difference between the two breweries was that Eastpoint was
privately owned, while Oyster City was more corporate.

"I can't tell you how relieved I am you're here. As a manager
under a corporate umbrella, I didn't know how to handle these
protection payments. I was too scared not to pay them. They
knew my whole family's names, but I couldn't tell corporate
either. So, I've hidden the payments as maintenance costs in
the books. If they audit me, I'll be fired. I'm in a difficult
position."

"I get it. This will all be over soon. Just play the game, and I
promise I'll nail them. My friend in the FBI is seeking RICO
charges. If that occurs, they won't see the light of day once
convicted. I won't need you to testify. I have enough on him
already. I wouldn't want to put you or your family in harm's
way," said Rick, giving her a reassuring smile.

She thanked him profusely and handed him a handful of
free beer coupons, which he declined but accepted for
Boudreaux later.

to use another day, and they left. Rick texted Jules to pick
him up at the bookstore. He knew she loved that place, and he
could kill a few minutes there waiting for her.

FIFTEEN

Carson had his team ready. Rick received permission from Jake to use one of his beach house rentals for the operation, which included a full tactical team, forensic accountants, and investigators. The plan was to hit the warehouse at 5:00 a.m. Possum handled their meals that night, while Rick drove them over in his Bronco, entering the garage and closing the door behind him. After dinner, he went over a blueprint of the warehouse, detailing where to find what he had already photographed. Though his evidence findings couldn't be used in court, the same evidence collected with a warrant would be admissible.

Rick left the meeting around 9:10 p.m. and called Gary, arranging for him to fly Jake and Cindy back as soon as the arrest warrants were served. The FBI would move fast; they were already aware of the evidence Rick had found and needed hard copies. The federal judge was poised to sign the arrest warrants as soon as they retrieved the documents from the warehouse. Rick wanted to participate in the raid, but he wasn't authorized to do so. Sleep came hard that night as he worried about Carson's safety, hoping everything would go as planned. Carson promised to text him if they were successful.

~

At 4:15 a.m., five black SUVs traveled down the two-track road to the warehouse. The FBI SWAT team led the charge; one agent was stationed by the breaker box at the property's edge, waiting for the signal. The SWAT team locked and loaded, then gave him the go-ahead. He flipped the breaker, plunging the outside lights into darkness. Moments later, one of the guards exited the building.

Upon seeing the chaos, the lead SWAT agent yelled, "Down on the ground. Now!"

The guard, illuminated by the red LED lights from the rifle scopes, dropped to the ground without uttering a word. Two special agents seized him and dragged him off in handcuffs. Although he was not officially arrested, he was detained for questioning.

The second guard was not so fortunate. He emerged from the building in response to the commotion and began shooting. Agents returned fire, neutralizing him in mere seconds. Although taking a life wasn't part of the plan, it expedited the arrest warrant process. The team rushed into the warehouse, collecting boxes of documents, all computers, surveillance hard drives, and everything else necessary to secure arrest warrants. They cordoned off the area, with several agents remaining on-site for a day or two.

Once the SUVs were packed with evidence, Carson texted Rick:

We got it. All of it. One guard killed. No agents harmed.

Thank God. See you soon. Glad you're safe.

Rick informed the team, who had all risen early with a mix of apprehension and excitement about the mission. An hour later, Carson arrived at Jake's beach house, a big smile on his face.

"We did it! Great team effort! Lobsters on me!" exclaimed Carson.

"This is an oyster town, but I'm sure we can score some lobsters. We should grill up some oysters for appetizers too—what's it called?" said Rick.

"Oysters Rockefeller. Maybe we should have breakfast first; it's only 7:45 a.m.," laughed Possum.

"Please, please, please make your biscuits with sausage gravy!" begged Rick.

"Alright, I don't mind."

Rick brewed another cup of coffee while Jules settled on the back deck, beginning a book she had picked up, *Bonded In Flame* by a new author named Lily Stoneheart. Though she was not usually a romance reader, this was a romantasy with paranormal elements, fantastic worlds, dragons, and a forbidden love story. She was excited to dive in.

Rick sipped his coffee, watching the amazing Possum in the kitchen. He asked Malia for help with the dough, knowing she was an excellent cook. It warmed his heart to see Possum happy; Malia had transformed his life after the loss of his wife.

Just then, a loud pounding echoed through the house.

"Rick! Rick! Open up!" came a frantic voice from outside.

Rick sprinted to the door, seeing it was Peter, head of the security team.

"Y'all have to get out of here now. Immediately."

"What?! Why?!"

"No time to explain. Exit the house—now! I'm serious. Forget your stuff and come with me!" Peter yelled.

Rick ran to grab Jules as Possum and Malia bolted past them, just before Carson. They had just made it outside when a whistling sound sliced through the air.

The house exploded.

Kaboom!

They reached the edge of the driveway just as a missile punched through the roof. With no warning and no time to pack, the warhead detonated inside the house. The entire structure lifted slightly off its foundation, followed by windows shattering in perfect circles of glass. A split second later, flames belched out of every opening—doors, windows, and the new hole in the roof, an orange and white eruption bright enough to hurt their eyes.

The blast wave hit them next, shoving them forward with force, hot and dense like an oven door opening in their faces. Ears popped as dust and debris stung their skin. They stood in shock, ringing ears muffling the chaos around them.

Roof tiles, chunks of siding, and splintered beams hurtled past, clattering down the street. The garage door buckled outward, slamming flat onto the lawn, and the Bronco erupted into flames. A smaller boom followed, sharp and nearly gunshot-like, from a ruptured gas line, sending another flame tongue through the wreckage.

In thirty seconds, it was over. The house sagged into itself, flames licking at the remnants, with black smoke spiraling into the cold morning air. All that remained was heat, the smell of burning wood and plastic, and the low crackle of what used to be a home.

Rick wrapped his arms around Jules, who, like everyone else, was covered in ash.

"Are you okay, Jules?"

She looked stunned, as did they all. Rick noticed Possum crouched, holding his leg; a significant piece of wood protruded from his upper right thigh.

"I'm not hurt—help Possum!" yelled Jules.

Rick unsteadily got to his feet, head pounding, as if someone had wrapped a pillow around his ears and duct-taped it.

"Possum, how bad is it?"

The wood shard was about two inches wide and ten inches long, embedded in his thigh.

"We gotta get that out. Are you ready?" Rick asked.

Possum nodded but said nothing.

"This is gonna hurt like a mofo. On three. One, two..." Rick yanked the wood from Possum's leg.

Possum screamed in agony as Rick hastily took off his belt to wrap it around the wound and stop the bleeding. He took stock of everyone's injuries next.

In the chaos, Rick hadn't realized he was hurt too. Possum pointed at Rick's side.

"Dude, you're bleeding."

Rick unbuttoned his shirt and discovered glass protruding from his flank. He reached down and pulled it out. It was small, and he managed to pull it out intact. Then a shocking thought hit him: *The pets! Chief and Choco. Oh my God.*

"Rick, they were in the backyard on the deck," said Jules.

Rick ran as fast as he could, leaving a trail of blood droplets in his wake. When he reached the fence gate, which was ablaze, he kicked it open and dashed into the backyard. He spotted Choco sitting by the back fence, licking at his paw.

Rushing over, Rick noticed the splinter of glass embedded

in it, which he gently pulled out, checking for other injuries. Choco seemed unharmed.

Rick scanned for Chief and saw his PVC perch lying on the deck. Chief was nowhere in sight. Then he noticed feathers floating in the pool, and his heart dropped as he saw Chief face down in the water.

Without a second thought, he dove in and pulled Chief out. The bird was motionless.

"Oh my God! No!" cried Rick, feeling for a heartbeat—nothing.

Could a bird even receive CPR? He had to try. Wading to the pool deck, he placed Chief on it, wrapping his mouth around the bird's beak, blowing gently. With two fingers, he pressed on Chief's chest.

Jules knelt beside him, crying uncontrollably.

"Is he dead?" she asked, tears streaming down her face.

"I have to save him!" Rick insisted.

He continued to breathe for Chief as Jules bowed her head and clasped her hands in prayer, reciting the Lord's Prayer and begging God to spare Chief's life.

Rick persisted for several tense minutes, nearly giving up when, suddenly, water rushed from Chief's beak. The bird's head popped up, and he began shaking himself dry like a dog. Flapping his wings, Chief found his feet. Rick scooped him up and hugged him tight.

"Thank you, God, for saving Chief!"

Jules rushed over, and they all embraced in relief.

But then Rick's fear morphed into fury. "That motherfucker's gonna pay! Fuck the justice system. I'll deliver justice myself," he declared, a ferocity Jules had never seen from him before.

Sirens approached as the fire consumed the house. A fire

truck and ambulance arrived, firefighters extinguishing the blaze with massive amounts of water. Rick found Peter, urgency in his tone.

"What was it, Peter?"

"Stingers—shoulder-launched guided missiles. We received intel that one went missing during a training mission at Eglin Air Force Base. They intercepted chatter indicating it was tracked on its way to St. George Island. The idiots who stole it didn't realize they have built-in tracking devices. The military unit came to retrieve them, and we caught wind of it through our inside sources. A team's on the way now."

Two ambulances pulled up to the curb with EMTs hopping out. They checked Possum's vitals and placed him on a gurney. Malia, uninjured, drove with him in the ambulance; Rick realized he was still bleeding from his side, getting woozy from lost blood.

"Rick, you don't look so good."

Just as Peter stated that, everything went black, and Rick passed out.

The beeping of a heart monitor stirred Rick awake. When he opened his eyes, the first sight was Jules's beautiful face, worry etched in her features.

"Where am I?" he managed to croak.

"You're at Tallahassee Memorial Hospital."

"Tallahassee?"

"Yeah, we're all here. Possum's in another room; he just had surgery on his leg. The wood caused severe damage to his right vastus lateralis."

"His what?"

"His right outer quad muscle. They had to rebuild it and reattach some ligaments. He's not gonna be able to walk for a while, but he should recover with physical therapy," Jules explained.

"Where are Chief and Choco?"

"They are with Peter. The whole team moved to an undisclosed location. There are police guards outside your door and Possum's too. Carson is with Peter, gathering a team to arrest the entire organization."

"When?"

"Tonight."

"I gotta get out of here. I want in on this. That piece of shit tried to kill my team, my family. I have to be there."

"Rick, you're still out of it. You lost a ton of blood. You were basically in a coma until a few minutes ago. The team can handle it."

Rick tried to sit up and felt dizzy; Jules was right. As daylight streamed through the window, he realized he had time to recover before the raid.

"I need to talk to Carson," Rick insisted.

Jules fished Rick's phone from her purse, which she had taken during the ambulance ride. "Go ahead, Mr. Stubborn!" she tossed it to him, exasperated.

Though she was still annoyed, Rick understood the urgency of his situation. Carson answered by the third ring.

"Rick! You're alive. I was worried! Jules told me what the doctor said—hypovolemic shock from blood loss. You were very lucky. Thankfully, you have a common blood type, and they were able to get some back in you before it was too late. You need to rest."

"Fuck that! I want to be on the arrest team. I demand it."

"Calm down, bucko. This is a federal charge, now

compounded with domestic terrorism for the theft and use of military weapons. They found the stinger—it was tossed in the grass at the base of the bridge. We found one of Vito's capos' DNA on it; he will spend the rest of his life in prison."

"I don't give a fuck what you have to do. Can't you deputize me or something?"

"I see you are not gonna let this go. Let me make some calls. I might be able to pull some strings. How would you feel about becoming a Deputy U.S. Marshal?"

"If that will allow me to go on the bust, you can give me any title you want. U.S. Marshal sounds sexy, though," Rick joked.

"Okay, rest up, and I'll call you back."

"Thanks, Carson."

"U.S. Federal Marshal?" Jules chimed, her anger dissipating. "Will you get a uniform? You know I love a man in uniform."

She was warming to the idea of Rick going on the raid. While she wanted to participate too, she knew Rick wouldn't allow it. Instead, she opted for a more accommodating stance, unusual for her.

"A badge at least. Not sure about the uniform."

"Ooh, a badge and a gun? Now I'm turned on!" she laughed.

"Stop, come here, baby."

She moved closer, and Rick took her hand.

"I love you. You know I have to do this. I promise to stay safe. There will be a fucking army there. I just wanna see him go down. You get it?"

"I understand, Rick. It's okay. If the doctor gives you the all clear, it's fine by me. But if you get shot, I'm gonna fucking kill you!"

"Yes, ma'am. Fair enough. I won't get shot. I need to call Boudreaux."

"Hi, Rick! How are you?" Boudreaux's voice came through. "I heard what happened."

"I'm a little groggy and sore, but I'll be okay. Possum's gonna need therapy for his leg; he took a 2x4 to it, well, a piece of one anyway."

"I didn't know dey were planning that. I overheard Johnny Boy, one of Vito's capos, bragging about firing de missile. Dey definitely did it."

"He won't be bragging for long. They got his DNA off the stinger. He's done. Carson is planning a raid on the warehouse tonight. Will they all be there?"

"Yeah. There's a 6:00 p.m. meeting scheduled; dey are planning something big. I'm supposed to be there—it's mandatory."

"Don't be. As a matter of fact, you can head back to Mississippi. You've been critical in helping us with this case, but it's about to wrap up, and I'd rather you be safe. Get the hell out."

"You sure?" Boudreaux asked, a little uncertain.

"Yeah, just head back to the Tallahassee airport; I'll have a ticket waiting for you at Delta."

"Thanks, Rick! Keep me posted."

"Will do. Stay safe."

Rick felt good about getting Boudreaux out of harm's way. Now he needed to see the doctor and get his discharge from the hospital. He rang the nurse call button, and she arrived after a few minutes.

"Yes, Mr. Waters, what can I do for you?"

"Can I see the doctor? I need to get out of here."

"He's on rounds right now; let me see if I can locate him," she responded.

Rick sat upright in bed, no longer feeling dizzy. He swung his feet to the ground, taking a few steps while being careful with the IV line stuck in his arm. Feeling confident he would be alright to go on the raid, he settled back on the edge of the bed.

A little while later, the doctor arrived.

"Mr. Waters, I'm Dr. Vikram Patel. The nurse informs me you'd like to be discharged. I highly advise against it, but I can't stop you."

"I understand, Doctor, but I must get out. It's urgent."

The doctor checked Rick's chart and vitals before continuing.

"Okay, I wouldn't go jogging or anything, but I'll sign the discharge papers. I recommend you go home or to a friend's place and rest."

"No home left—blown to smithereens, didn't you hear?"

"Oh yes; I'm sorry. Go to a hotel or a friend's then—rest, drink lots of fluids, and eat a steak. You need the iron."

"Thank you, doctor. A steak sounds great."

The doctor left, and about half an hour later, a hospital administrator arrived with discharge papers for Rick to sign. A police officer escorted him to Possum's room.

"Hey, buddy! How's the leg?" Rick asked, hugging Possum and Malia.

"Kinda like those chicken breasts I tenderize after beating the shit out of them with a meat mallet."

"Yikes, very creative description."

"You're getting out of here?"

"Yes, they're serving the arrest warrants tonight. I want to be there."

"Can you use your Meta Ray Bans and stream it live on your Facebook profile? I'd go, but a guy in a wheelchair would probably just get in the way. By the way, Malia called Gary and let him know what happened."

"Oh, good! Streaming it is a great idea. I'll set the privacy settings for just the team so Gary and Jake can watch too. I'll text them a heads-up. Guess what?"

"What?"

"They're deputizing me as a U.S. Marshal."

"Damn, that's cool, man! Nice to know people in the right places."

"Yep, Cason is awesome. Alright, we're gonna find a nice hotel nearby and rest until Carson tells me to head out. I'll book you a room too, Malia."

"I appreciate it, but no need. I'm gonna stay here with Possum."

That made Rick smile.

"Okay, if you change your mind or when they let Possum out of here, have him text me, and I'll get a room near ours."

"Thank you, Rick."

Jules and Rick were escorted out, and one of the deputies gave them a ride to an Enterprise Rental location. Once they had their rental secured, Rick told the deputy he was fine on his own. The deputy told Rick to call him if he needed anything, then handed him his business card. Jules booked a room at the Hotel Duval, downtown.

CHAPTER
SIXTEEN

As Rick drove toward the hotel, his stomach growled, reminding him of the hearty breakfast Possum was preparing when they had to evacuate. Steak sounded perfect right about now.

"You hungry?" he asked Jules.

"Does a bear eat in the woods?" she replied, a playful grin on her face.

"Uhh, I suppose so," Rick chuckled.

"There's a great steakhouse, Connors Steak & Seafood, just off I-10. It's only about six miles from here. I stumbled upon it once while getting gas. It rocks!" exclaimed Rick, enthusiasm returning.

"Yay! Cow! I'm starving. Can we have a couple of steaks delivered to Possum and Malia?" Jules asked.

"Yeah, I don't see why not. They're probably famished too."

The hostess seated them in a booth, and as Rick scanned the menu, a wave of anxiety washed over him. The reality of having survived a missile attack hit like a ton of bricks. He glanced at Jules, gripping her hand tightly, and ordered a bottle of St. Regis Cabernet—the only non-alcoholic red wine on the list. Jules noticed his anxiety, particularly evident in his breathing.

"Damn, I wish I had my Buzz Drops," he muttered.

Jules beamed and pulled a bottle from her purse, sliding it toward him along with a Xanax. Just seeing it helped calm his nerves.

"I took the other half," she admitted.

Once their server poured the wine, Rick added a few drops of the calming liquid. "What are you gonna order?" he asked.

"I think I'm gonna go with the ribeye. You?"

I'm gonna get the hanger steak. I read they have to have the most iron."

"That's in the skirt steak family?"

"Very good, Jules."

"I know my cow," she grinned back.

After their late lunch and early dinner, they checked into the hotel. Rick took a much-needed shower while Jules flipped through the TV channels. She had dropped her book during their hasty exit, and their belongings were likely destroyed. Fortunately, both used Apple products, keeping their data secure in the cloud. They could upgrade their devices once the case was resolved, maybe even buy a new Bronco or Jeep later on. For now, Jules' vehicle would suffice.

"God, that feels better! Glad we grabbed those tooth-brushes from the front desk too," Rick said as he emerged.

"You're all clean and shiny now," she replied teasingly. "Now all we need is clean clothes."

"Shit! I forgot."

"I have a plan. Give me the keys. I'll be back in half an hour. Trust me," she said, determination in her eyes.

"Okay, baby. I trust you."

A few minutes after Rick finished showering, his phone whistled with a text from Carson.

Rick, can you meet us at the address I'm about to text you at 4:45 p.m.? I need to deputize you before we hit the warehouse legally.

Rick glanced at his watch—it was just 2:15 p.m.

Yes, I'll be there.

It would take less than an hour and a half to reach the meeting point. As long as he left by 3:00 p.m., he'd be golden. He texted Jules to make sure she'd be back in time. The Xanax made him drowsy, and he laid his head on the pillow for a quick nap.

Jules opened the hotel door, waking him. He checked his watch again—it was 2:45 p.m.

"I got you some jeans, a fishing shirt, and clean underwear from Academy," she said, handing him the bags.

"Thank you so much! I need to throw these on and haul ass."

"Malia called to thank us for the steaks. Possum was super happy."

"Sweet," Rick said as he slipped into his jeans. Jules cleaned off his shoes in the bathroom, aware he would likely muddy them on the raid anyway.

Once dressed, Jules embraced him tightly, planting a kiss on his lips. Rick promised her he'd be safe before heading down to the rental car. He left at 2:59 p.m.

The FBI SWAT team gathered as Carson read from a script on

his iPad. The Deputy Attorney General monitored to ensure everything was legal.

"By the power granted to me by the USMS and the Deputy Attorney General, I hereby grant Rick Waters special temporary status as a U.S. Marshal, with all the jurisdiction and authority that comes with the badge. Congratulations, Rick."

Applause broke out as Carson hung the chain with the badge in a leather holster around Rick's neck. The DAG delivered a few words, punctuating Rick's new status with a formal touch. He was beaming.

"How temporary is this?" he murmured to Carson.

"It's meant for this mission, but I left it open-ended. We can discuss it later."

They reviewed the plan to issue the arrest warrants. The team had enough automatic weapons to take down a small army. Rick received an M4A1, a fully automatic version of the M4 carbine, along with a Beretta 9mm. Clad in bulletproof vests and armed with plenty of extra ammo, they were ready.

"Are we ready to do this?" Carson asked.

With a resounding "hoorah," they left the safe house, a short drive to the warehouse ahead. A dozen gangster cars were parked outside, hinting all might be inside—perfect for a complete takedown.

To flank the warehouse, Rick positioned himself by a tree for a steady shot if needed. His instincts urged him to unleash gunfire, but he knew he'd only fire if attacked first. The lead man on the SWAT team took position behind one of the Capos' cars and lifted his megaphone.

"Come out with your hands up! This is a federal arrest warrant. The warehouse is surrounded!" he shouted through the bullhorn.

All he got was silence in return. He repeated his warning. Still nothing. He waved over two of the men with a battering ram. They carefully approached the door. Rick took his rifle off safety. The man repeated his demand that they come out. They were again met with silence. He motioned to the men to break down the door. As the men pulled back the ram to bust it down Rick's phone buzzed on silent. He looked at it, and it was a text from Boudreaux.

It's a trap. It's gonna explode!

As Rick looked back toward the warehouse he yelled, "Stop!"

But it was too late. Everything went white; the warehouse exploded, killing the three agents closest to the blast. Cars flipped, and debris flew, showering the area. Rick and Carson, positioned safely away, felt the shockwave but were spared. The sight was horrific—body parts and pieces of debris littering the ground, a massacre.

Carson immediately called in a medevac chopper, rushing to assess the injured. After a moment, once Rick caught his breath, he texted Jules:

It was a booby trap. Several agents are dead. Carson and I are uninjured.

Oh my God! was her quick reply.

Rick helped however he could, tending to the wounded agents. The federal government would come down hard now, leaving nowhere for the gangsters to hide. The loss of lives weighed heavily on the team, a burden Rick felt acutely.

Once the chaos settled, Rick followed Carson back—was there really any place left that would feel safe?

"What now?" he asked, eyes narrowing with resolve.

"We hunt them down like the rats they are. Can Boudreaux track them?"

"He's at the airport heading back to Mississippi. Let me call him."

Rick reached for his phone, only to see Boudreaux's message pop up:

I didn't get on my flight. Are you okay?

"Boudreaux! Where are you?" Rick asked as he connected the call.

"I'm back at the rental car agency to get my Denali. What happened?"

"It was horrific. Three dead special agents, two in critical condition, and several more severely injured. Carson and I were far enough away that we weren't hit."

"Thank God you're okay. I'm sick to hear about the dead agents; that's terrible."

"Listen, I know I said you could leave, but..."

"I'm on it, Rick. The worst part is that now I have to meet them and pretend to celebrate what they've done. It will take all my strength to fake it. I will get a message to you as soon as I can about where they are hiding. I'm working on a plan to get them all together."

"Great, we'll be standing by," Rick replied.

"Boudreaux is gonna try to get them all together in one place. I'm gonna head back to Tallahassee. I'll keep you posted. I need to find us a safer place closer. I'll take Choco and Chief with me. Jules will be happy."

"I'm working on finding a place," said Carson.

Rick left and started driving toward Tallahassee. He was sick to his stomach thinking about the body parts he had seen on the ground. He had just talked to those men. Their families would be devastated. He couldn't wait to get back and hold Jules in his arms. He stopped at a pet store, picking up a large kennel and a sleeping pad for Choco, a perch, bird pellets, and a cat kennel for Chief. He snuck the supplies into the hotel with a cart, careful to avoid attention.

"Hi, Chief," Jules said. "Oh look, his feathers are singed at the ends."

"He's one lucky bird."

"Lucky his daddy doesn't mind kissing the beak of a bird. You saved his life, Rick."

"You would've done the same thing," he countered.

"Damn right I would!"

Jules wrapped her arms around Rick earnestly. "I'm so glad you're okay. I'm sorry you had to see those men get killed; that must've been hard."

"Extremely. We'll get them though. Boudreaux has a plan."

"Come here, Choco. Sit down, boy," she called as she played with the dog.

Rick took care of the kennels he had just purchased. They came in large boxes but required no tools to assemble, luckily. The perch was a thick T-branch attached to a base on wheels, which cost nearly a hundred and fifty dollars—highway robbery, but Chief was worth it.

"We need to get closer to Apalachicola, but somewhere safe. Carson's working on that. We can stay here tonight and see what he finds. I'm exhausted," Rick said, plopping down on the bed's edge.

"I know, baby. Let's relax in bed with our two boys and watch TV."

Rick slipped under the comforter as Chief waddled to tuck his head under Rick's chin. Choco jumped up to lay at the foot of the bed, while Jules snuggled against Rick. They turned on the TV, lost in a mindless show, and before long, Rick dozed off.

Jules fed Choco and watched as he climbed into his sleep kennel, a routine now familiar. Chief settled contentedly under

Rick's chin. Jules snapped a couple of photos, capturing the moment before climbing back into bed. They all slept soundly through the night.

The next morning, Jules woke before Rick and made a pot of coffee. She snuck out to grab him a Danish from the hotel kitchen, returning with bear claws—his favorite treat.

"Good morning, sleepyhead! I have bear claws!" she announced, excitement in her voice.

"Oh my God, I love you!" he replied, devouring one without even sipping his coffee.

After finishing a second claw, he joined her at the wet bar. The hotel they booked had no balcony, but the Diamond Suite included a separate room with a bar and high-top chairs. They chatted about their dreams of escaping to the Everglades once this case was over—planning on taking their motorhome south with Choco and Chief in tow, blending into their cozy little family.

Rick received a text from Carson with an address for a safe house available after 5:00 p.m., once the team had scouted the area.

"We should check on Possum," Rick suggested.

"Yep, I agree. I'll put the do-not-disturb sign on the door and the pets in their kennels. I'll leave the TV on in case Chief decides to make any noise."

SEVENTEEN

"Hey buddy. How you feeling?" Rick asked as he entered Possum's hospital room.

"Not too bad. The leg is still painful, but I got some good drugs. Malia told me what happened. That was rough. I'm glad you and Carson are okay. Listen, I'm getting out of here today. I guess I can get a room or something."

"How about I hire a car and have them drive you and Malia home to Destin? We could really use your computer expertise, and at least you'll have your iMac there since your MacBook was destroyed. What do you say?" Rick suggested.

"I'm supposed to start physical therapy soon."

"Even better! We can arrange for it to be done at your condo. A private therapist could come to you. Deal?"

"Sounds good, Rick. Thank you. I uploaded all the files I took from the warehouse. I can go over them with a fine-toothed comb and make sure everyone involved pays the price."

"That's what I'm talking about!"

Rick arranged for a driver for Possum and Malia while Possum completed his discharge paperwork. He thanked the medical staff for all they had done, and soon they were on their way to Destin.

It was a little after midday, and they decided to go tech shopping. Rick checked online and found there wasn't an Apple Store in Tallahassee, but there was a Best Buy. That would have to do. They drove over, and Rick entered the store with a sense of purpose.

"Hello, my man. Are you ready to make some nice commissions?" he asked the young sales associate.

"Well, we don't work on commission at Best Buy, but I'm happy to help you, sir," the young man replied.

"That's tragic! Okay, if you can steer me in the best direction, I'll take good care of you," Rick said with a grin.

"We both need all new devices. Our old ones are no more," Rick explained.

"Are they all on the cloud?" the associate asked.

"They were indeed. We still have our phones, but that's it. I'd also like to upgrade those too," Rick clarified.

"Are you completely Apple, or a mix of both? We have some great Windows PCs these days, too," the salesman said.

"We're Apple all the way."

"Oh, great. That'll make it easier for me to help you synchronize it all to where you left off. We've got fast Wi-Fi here, so it won't take too long," the associate assured him.

"What's your fastest 13 to 15-inch MacBook these days?"

"If you want compact, I'd recommend the 13-inch MacBook Air with the M4 chip. If you want blazing speed, I'd go for the 16-inch MacBook Pro with the M1 Max chip. It's a bit cumbersome to carry around, but it's smoking fast."

"Okay, I'll go for the 13. We travel a lot. Jules?"

"Yeah, me too," she replied with a smile.

"Now do you need an iPad?" he continued.

"Yep. What do you suggest?" asked Rick.

"I'd recommend the 11th Gen iPad. You could go with the Pro, but since you have MacBooks, it's honestly a waste of money."

Rick began piling up the boxes. "Okay, what's the newest iPhone?"

"The 17 Pro. They have the Pro and Pro Max. It's mostly a size difference—6.3 inches versus 6.9 for the Max."

"I'll go with the Pro Max. Jules probably wants the Pro, right?"

Jules nodded in agreement, and they both picked out their favorite colors, along with some nice OtterBoxes.

"Do you need any backpacks or laptop bags?" the salesman asked.

"Great idea. Actually, we'll need a couple of those iPad cases with built-in keyboards. I'm good on backpacks, though," Rick replied.

"That's it then. Do you want the extended insurance warranty coverage on all of it?"

"Do you get to keep any of that money?" Rick asked.

"Not commission-wise, but we do have bonuses and incentives from the company to push those. Honestly, they're really good coverage. It's completely up to you."

"I normally don't get those, but if I had, my burned-up MacBook would've been replaced for free. Plus, it sounds like it helps you overall with the company. Sign me up for the max. Are you in school, son?"

"Yes, sir. I go to FSU. I'm studying Criminal Psychology. I want to be an FBI profiler or something similar."

"Well, this is your lucky day, son. I'm a private detective, and one of my best friends, Carson, was one of the FBI's top profilers back in the day. He worked on the Ted Bundy, Night Stalker, and Green River Killer cases, among others. After you graduate, I can have him put in a good word for you. If you want to get some real-life experience, you could intern with us in Destin during the summer break."

"Carson Peters? The Carson Peters, the great profiler I've studied in school?" Charlie's eyes widened.

"That's him. You wanna meet him?"

"Here's my card. Put your name and number in my new phone you're setting up, and I'll arrange a meeting. It's Charlie, right?"

"Yes, sir. I'm Charlie Bronson from Fort Walton Beach, and I'd love to intern over summer break."

"Charles Bronson?" Rick laughed.

"My friend says that, but it's actually Charlie. I'll answer to either. They get a kick out of it."

"Small world, Charlie. Ring it all up and I'll holler at Carson for you later. He'd love to meet someone who studied him. His head will get too big for his neck to support it. Ha-ha."

Charlie rang everything up, and Rick paid with his platinum card. While waiting for the cloud sync to finish, Rick found another salesman and asked him if he had an envelope. The man returned with a small white envelope from the back office.

Rick put a thousand dollars in hundreds inside it, along with one of his business cards, and thanked the kid. As soon as the sync was complete, Charlie found Rick and handed him all his new devices.

"My phone number is there, sir, under Charles Bronson with (Charlie) in parentheses, so you won't forget it."

"Thanks, Charlie. Are you on a scholarship?"

"No, sir. That's why I work here."

"I see. Well, I know you don't get commission, so here's a little donation for school. Hurry up and put it in your pocket before your boss sees it. Open it later. I'll text you Carson's number after I talk to him, and he can arrange a meet-up. He might even give you a tour of the crime lab in Quantico someday, too."

"Oh my God. Thank you, thank you! I don't know what to say."

"No need to say anything. Just study hard and keep your dreams alive, Charlie."

"Thank you, Mr. Waters. You made my year!"

Rick laughed, patting him on the shoulder as they left the store. He was eager to tell Carson about Charlie; he had mentioned considering mentoring someone, and Charlie seemed like an excellent candidate.

They loaded their new gear into the rental car and headed toward Apalachicola. On the way, Rick spotted a used car dealership and saw a maroon 4-door Jeep that caught his eye. It had a star on the hood and already had a Blue Ox tow bar installed under the bumper. He pulled in.

A salesman approached quickly, inspecting the windows. "Good eyes! That's one of the nicest Jeeps on the lot. It's the Jeep Wrangler Freedom Edition, specifically the Oscar Mike version—built for those always on the go. An old lady named it Sadie when she traded it in. She hated to let it go and rarely drove it. It's in mint condition."

"Spare me the used car sales schtick. What's your absolute rock-bottom cash deal on this thing? You have one shot at it. I can have the money wired today if you take care of me?" Rick said assertively.

The salesman appeared flustered and handed Rick the keys. "Take her for a test drive, and I'll talk to my manager."

Rick and Jules climbed in. The seats featured a large star embroidered on them, just like the hood. It was a sharp-looking Jeep. They pulled out and drove up the street, Rick switching it into four-wheel drive. Everything was in perfect working order. Though it didn't ride as smoothly as his Bronco, the oversized custom Fuel wheels and three-inch lift kit made up for it. The Jeep had excellent stance, and the existing Blue Ox tow bar was a major selling point.

They returned to the parking lot, and the salesman greeted them. "This is the best I can do," he said, handing Rick a piece of paper with the price breakdown.

The price was reasonable, especially with a three-year extended warranty included. Rick knew Jeeps maintained their value, and he recognized this one could sell for much more than the listed price.

"Okay, I'll give you a cash deposit now and have the balance wired to you," said Rick confidently.

"Yes, sir. I'll get the paperwork ready."

Rick planned to keep the Jeep for a while, possibly making some aftermarket upgrades to it before reselling. He'd probably order a new Bronco once the insurance money came through, but for now, the Jeep would work perfectly for toting it behind the motorhome. He was ready to get out of Dodge.

After finalizing the purchase, they drove to the safe house near Apalachicola. Rick texted Carson that they were pulling in, and security let them through.

"Hi, Carson. Any developments?" Rick asked as he joined the team.

"I've assembled a new crew. We are using every means at

our disposal to find them. I still think our best bet is for Boudreaux to provide a location. Time will tell," Carson replied.

Rick stayed up talking with Carson and the team for a while, but Jules, exhausted, retreated to the bedroom to read. Rick eventually joined her, and they snuggled until they both fell asleep.

CHAPTER
EIGHTEEN

Boudreaux paced back and forth in his hotel room, anxiety gnawing at him. He had left a message with an old friend, Matthew Leroux, an actor based in New Orleans. Matthew had a background in Broadway and independent films, yet the fact that he wasn't a huge star by now always amazed Boudreaux. He was a method actor, immersing himself completely in any role he took on.

. When he studied for a part, he became the character. That's how they met. Boudreaux was known in the Bywater area of New Orleans as a gangster. They all knew he worked for the Cajun Connection. It was no secret. Even the local police steered clear of him mostly. But not Matthew. He had gotten a part in a mob movie, and he immersed himself in the role. So much so that he approached Boudreaux as the character, it nearly cost him his life. He was playing the part of hitman Tony "The Hammer" Gerardo.

In a Bywater bar, he pulled up a bar stool beside Boudreaux and, over a beer or two, ingratiated himself to Boudreaux. He mentioned that he had a job and needed some help. Boudreaux remembered that day as if it were yesterday.

"I understand you have connections. I have a job you might be interested in," Matthew had said, casually leaning against the bar.

"Oh yeah? What kind of job?" Boudreaux asked, intrigued.

"I need to make someone go away. I'm getting fifty grand for the hit, but it's delicate and I need someone I can trust. I'll split it with you."

Boudreaux raised an eyebrow, taking a sip of his beer. "Who's the target?"

"Ray Nagin," Matthew replied.

"The mayor?" Boudreaux was shocked.

"Yeah, that's right. He's in Dallas now. The way he handled Katrina has rubbed some people the wrong way."

"Some people? I'd kill that cockroach for free. Count me in."

After a few more beers, they moved to the courtyard behind the bar and discussed the hit. Matthew kept up the act, going so far as to give Boudreaux a fake Dallas address. At the end, before they parted ways, he confessed to Boudreaux that he was just working on a part and needed to get close to a real wise guy. Boudreaux pulled his gun on him and stuck it in his mouth and nearly pulled the trigger. It was a life-or-death moment. Then he thought about how well Matthew had played the part and began to laugh. They became close friends after that.

Boudreaux's plan was for Matthew to contact Vito, pretend to be one of the capos in the Cajun Connection, and tell Vito that he, along with half a dozen of his men, wanted to leave New Orleans and join Vito's crew. Then Boudreaux could arrange a meeting and get all of Vito's crew in one location. It would be tricky, but to have a large number of one crime family join another would require that they all meet to feel each other out. It was a solid plan B, but Boudreaux He had called Matthew over an hour ago and was anxiously awaiting his return call. Cracking open a beer, he sat on the edge of the bed, counting the seconds until his phone rang. Just as he was about to open another beer, it buzzed.

"Thank God!" Boudreaux exclaimed.

"Hey Boudreaux, where are you?" Matthew's voice crackled through.

"I'm in New Orleans. Sorry I was on the subway when you called—reception was spotty. Tell me about this gig," Matthew said.

Boudreaux outlined the plan in detail, hoping Matthew could deliver.

"I love it. When do you want me to call him?" Matthew asked.

"Tonight. I'll have you call my phone, then I'll hand it over to him. You need to be this guy. Vito is no fool. If he suspects he's being played, it could backfire, and he'll come after me."

"I understand. Do you think he knows any names from the New Orleans crew?" Matthew questioned.

"No. You can be anyone you want."

"In that case, I'll be the Hammer. Doubt he's seen the movie I was in; fewer than twenty people saw it," Matthew chuckled.

"I know; we watched it in my apartment the day before the Super Bowl," Boudreaux replied, smiling at the memory.

"That's right! I got so drunk from doing shots because I was so nervous you wouldn't like it, then I ended up sleeping on the couch."

"Yeah, the good ol' days," Boudreaux reminisced.

Boudreaux ended the call and headed over to where Vito and some of the crew were hiding out. When he met with Vito, he wasn't as keen on the idea as he thought he would be. He was apprehensive. It was a tough time for them, though. He was still a candidate for Congress, but he was being sought by the FBI and was hiding out. No wonder he was nervous. To sweeten the deal, Boudreaux suggested to Vito that some of the crew come over and confess to the missile strike on the house, do the time, and take the heat off of Vito in exchange for a cash payment for their families. That was the story Vito wanted to head. He still believed he had a chance to win a seat in Congress, so diverting blame would help his campaign. At this point, he was only on the Feds' radar, and although he ran the entire Newark Crew, there was no solid evidence directly linking him to the girls' trafficking or the missile attack. The Feds were still building a case.

"Let's do it," Vito finally agreed.

"Okay, he'll call at 7:00 p.m. sharp on my phone, and then I can give you the phone or put him on speaker."

Vito nodded. He had bought Boudreaux's story. Now all Boudreaux had to do was wait. He returned to his hotel room and updated Matthew on the new twist he had to sell Vito on the phone. He took it in stride. His voice sounded different, and he was already in character. Over the years, he had grown used to Matthew morphing into different characters. If it was a big part, he would dress, talk, and use the name of the character he was going to play, sometimes months before filming started. He was a method actor through and through. It got annoying sometimes because he'd never break character. Boudreaux remembered a time he had taken part as an autistic man with Tourette's syndrome. He nearly got his ass kicked several times. Boudreaux stayed close to him throughout to protect him. Even when there was a threat of someone stomping his ass, he wouldn't break character. They were in a bar, and he yelled stupid bitch at a woman minding her own business. Her boyfriend was a monster of a man and came after Matthew. It took a lot of convincing from Boudreaux and the flash of his gun to get him to understand that Matthew was just playing a part for a movie and to back down, especially after Matthew called him a sleazy cunt in the weird, loud manner the character did. Boudreaux tried his best to keep him out of the public eye, but he portrayed that character for three weeks before filming started. It was a long three weeks.

"It's go time," Boudreaux whispered to himself as the clock neared his meeting with Vito.

Arriving at the hideout at 6:45 p.m., he noticed several men playing poker in the old fish house they were using as a base. Vito was in a separate room, puffing on a cigar. At exactly 7:00 p.m., Boudreaux's phone rang. He answered Matthew's call and handed the phone to Vito, straining to catch only Vito's side of the conversation. Vito's expression shifted to one of mild amusement as he listened.

and couldn't make out what Matthew was saying. Based on Vito's body language and eventual smile, he felt it was a good call. He couldn't act too excited, but he needed to know what Vito decided.

"We good?" asked Boudreaux.

"Yeah, we're good. They want to meet the entire crew in person. If this goes as planned, you will be promoted. You ever been made?"

Boudreaux's eyes widened in disbelief. "No, boss. I am beside myself. That's an incredible offer."

"It's on the table. We'll discuss it after the meeting."

"Thanks, boss."

Becoming a made man in a mafia organization was the equivalent of becoming a full partner in a prestigious law firm, but for different reasons. It meant a much higher share of the profits, and he would be untouchable by any of the other crew. It was something he had always dreamed of when he was back in the Cajun Connection, and for a moment, just a split second, he wanted to be made. But then he snapped out of it and remembered it was all fake. All just a ruse. Besides, he had stepped away from organized crime and had a new life now. A life he loved. He was playing a part in the same way that Matthew would be doing. It was all just an act.

Back at his hotel, Boudreaux called Matthew again to express his gratitude. He decided to send Matthew some money for his help, despite it being an informal agreement. He knew Matthew was dedicated, but he also knew that acting didn't always pay the bills.

even though he had done it for free. He was an actor, but he wasn't rich. He went for the lead role, but often he was in low-budget films, or he would take less to get the part because he believed in it so much. He was a dedicated thespian, but it didn't pay that well often times. Now all Boudreaux had to do was wait. They would meet in an old farm implement store that had been abandoned after it went out of business. Boudreaux couldn't wait to relay the news to Carson and Rick. He would call them soon, but first he wanted to blow off some steam and celebrate a little, plus he was famished and hadn't eaten anything all day. He strolled down to the Up The Creek Raw Bar, a nice little local watering hole and restaurant right on the Apalachicola River.

"Bingo, who wants to play?" a man announced over the microphone.

Bingo? Before he could decline, the attractive bartender slid a bingo card and a dabber over to him.

"Five dollars. It could be your lucky night," she said with a seductive wink.

He didn't really want to play, but she was one of the hottest women he'd seen in a long time, so he went along. After paying for the beer and tipping her five dollars for the first one, she became even more attentive to him. It had been a long time since he'd been with a woman, and she seemed interested. She may have been playing him for tips, but he was gonna try anyway. When bingo called B30 and Boudreaux won the $100, she came by and wrapped her arms around him to celebrate. She smelled amazing.

"I told you it could be your lucky night," she said.

"The night's still young. We'll see, huh?"

She knew what he meant, and she didn't shy away.

"You like Pimm's cups?" asked Boudreaux.

"I never heard of it. What is it?" she asked.

"Only de best drink to ever come out of New Orleans."

"New Orleans. I love that city. I went to Mardi Gras once."

"Darlin, dis is de real New Orleans. I can take dis Benjamin and get what I need to make de drink. I'm staying at de Waterfront Hotel and Marina. My balcony is a great place for a nightcap, Cher."

"Oh, you are so Cajun. I haven't been called Cher since I was in New Orleans. Okay, I get off at ten. What's your room number? My name is Shari, but you can call me Cher. She slid a piece of paper over to Boudreaux, and he wrote his name and room number on it and slid it back to her."

He told her he would see her later and headed back to his hotel. He made a quick run to the liquor store and got everything needed to make Pimm's Cups. Before he got involved with the Cajun Connection, he worked as a bartender at The

Napoleon in New Orleans and made so many Pimm's Cups over the years that the recipe was emblazoned in his brain.

He took a shower, put on some cologne, and waited. He made a Pimm's Cup for himself while he waited, making sure he still had it down pat. It tasted like the real New Orleans. At 10:15 p.m., there was a knock on his door. He opened it and let her in. She smelled so good. He quickly made her a Pimm's Cup, and they moved to the balcony. She told him she had moved to Apalachicola from Georgia and that she wanted to be a marine biologist, but real life had gotten in the way, and her dreams had fallen by the wayside, and now she was a bartender. She was only a few credits shy of graduating but didn't have the money to finish. They had chemistry. It was evident and palpable. After four or five Pimm's Cups, she abruptly stood up, stuck out her hand, and thanked him for the drinks. Boudreaux looked like a whipped puppy. She laughed out loud, undid the first button on her blouse, and said,

"Take me to bed or lose me forever."

CHAPTER
NINETEEN

A loud knock on the door roused Rick from sleep. It was Carson.

"Rick, I got a text from Boudreaux. It's going down."

Rick rubbed his eyes, still disoriented. "When?"

"Soon. Boudreaux said Vito had called a meeting with all his capos. Somehow, Boudreaux convinced Vito that some of the leadership in the Cajun Connection wanted to team up with Vito's crew to increase their strength. I think he made it all up. There is a meeting planned for this morning at 10:30 a.m. You wanna join us, Marshal?"

"You're damn right I'm going," Rick replied, adrenaline kicked in as he quickly changed.

He let Jules sleep in a bit. Quietly, he snuck out of the bedroom. The safehouse was in a bunker in the center of town. It was under the old jail, which was actually the Franklin County Courthouse and Jail. It had been shut down for many years, and from the outside it looked like a rundown, boarded-up relic. Underneath it, though, was a labyrinth of servers and other rooms that the government had set up as a data center during the A.I. craze. There were hundreds of data centers hidden in plain sight to protect them from antifa and other organizations that wanted to harm anything A.I. There wasn't even an entrance to the underground part of the facility inside the main building. A long tunnel led from under the old building to a private residence that housed a young couple who worked for the NSA. The house sat across the street from the old, abandoned jailhouse on the corner of Commerce and Leslie. There was a lot of street parking in the area, and tourists used it to walk down to the waterfront. To anyone walking by it looked like an old house and nothing more. But it had a trap-door under the floor that led to the catacombs beneath the old jailhouse.

Rick strapped on his weapons and bulletproof vest, ready for round two. He was concerned that if shooting broke out, Boudreaux might get caught in the crossfire. He needed to make sure Boudreaux was safe before they raided the meeting. The planned meeting would take place at the old implement center that had closed just off Highway 98 near Junction 385. It was heavily wooded, which would help the team approach without being detected so easily. They had an eye in the sky giving them aerial updates.

"You ready?" asked Carson.

"Ready as I'll ever be."

The FBI SWAT team was already in place when Rick and Carson arrived. Rick implored them to wait until he gave them the signal that Boudreaux was out of the building and safe. Boudreaux confirmed to Rick that Vito was inside and waiting for members of the Cajun Connection to arrive. There was no one coming. It was all a ruse set up by Boudreaux. Vito paced back and forth as he waited for the men to arrive. He was getting anxious and kept checking his watch. Cell service under the tin.-roofed building was weak You could get a text out, but making a call was tough. That was the story Boudreaux used to get out of the building.

"Boss, they should be here. Maybe they missed a tour. I'll step outside and try to call them. Can't get through in here," he suggested, easing Vito's tension.

Vito nodded and continued to pace. His goons were all at a big table playing cards and smoking. Boudreaux prewrote GO TIME on his text message to Rick and CarsonInside, the SWAT leader picked up his megaphone and declared, "Come out with your hands up! You are surrounded!" Silence greeted him. He repeated the command, but again received no reply.

demand. No one answered. Two teams on each side launched tear gas into the building, smashing through the crusty vented windows on top of the facility. Within minutes, they came rushing out of the building. Thick white plumes of tear gas poured from the shattered windows and open loading dock, drifting across the cracked asphalt in waves. Five men from Vito's crew, tough gangsters who believed the building could be defended, stumbled out the side exit in a ragged line. They coughed hard, eyes watering, bandanas pulled over their faces but now soaked with tears and snot.

"Hands up! Drop your weapons! On the ground!" yelled the SWAT team leader. Blaring through a bullhorn.

The perimeter was tight. FBI SWAT operators in full tactical gear, with black helmets and body armor, knelt behind ballistic shields, vehicle doors, and concrete barriers. M4 carbines and MP5 submachine guns followed every move, red dots flickering across the gangsters' chests like fireflies from hell. The lead Capo, a broad-shouldered enforcer named Rico with tattoos up his neck, blinked through the sting and raised his Glock anyway. Whether it was pride or stubbornness didn't matter.

"Fuck you!" he rasped, his voice raw from the gas, and fired two wild shots at the nearest agent, missing. The shots rang out, sparks flying as the window of a nearby car shattered. That was all it took. It was enough to set everything off instantaneously and overwhelmingly. A staccato of thunder erupted from the SWAT line—controlled bursts, precise and disciplined. Tracers streaked orange through the haze. Rico jerked backward as multiple rounds slammed into his chest and then higher, spinning him off his feet in a spray of red that mixed with the lingering gas. The man behind him, younger and panicked, tried to dive back toward the door but was hit in the legs. He screamed and fell hard, his AK-47 sliding across the pavement. Another gangster lowered his shotgun without firing, then raised it in defiance. He fell to his knees, gasping from the multiple holes in his body It was too late to negotiate. Another man swung a sawed-off shotgun toward the tree line, shouting obscenities through his burning throat. A sniper's bullet from the rooftop of a parked car across the parking lot hit his shoulder before he could fire; the loud crack would echo just after. He collapsed, the shotgun firing harmlessly into the ground. He was then showered with a barrage of bullets.

The last one out, Vito, threw his pistols down right away and put his hands behind his head, dropping to his knees as ordered.

"I'm done! I'm done!" he shouted, coughing. As an agent approached him with handcuffs, he reached behind his back, pulling a silver revolver from his waistband. The gun's shimmer reflected the sun. Rick put a red dot on his forehead before Vito could get the gun all the way around to the SWAT team member. His head reeled back when Rick took his shot. He was dead before he hit the ground.

In less than ten seconds, it was over. The gunfire faded, replaced by the hiss of settling gas and wind in the trees. The SWAT team moved forward in practiced formation, boots crunching on broken glass, zip-ties ready. They checked the downed gangsters for any signs of life. There was none.

"Scene secure," a calm voice said over the radio. "Suspects neutralized."

The warehouse released one last cloud of tear gas into the morning sky, as if it were relieved the ordeal was over. There would be no trial, no bail, no cameras in the courtroom. Justice was instantly served, and not a single wise guy survived. It was over. It was a bloodbath. The cop killers got what they deserved —instant karma.

Carson called in the second team to transport the bodies to the morgue. Sprinter vans arrived as officers began placing the deceased gangsters in body bags, the parking lot speckled with blood and shell casings. By midday, everything would be cleaned up, leaving the building to look as though nothing had ever happened.

Rick called Jules, who answered immediately. "Hey, baby, it's over. They're all dead."

"Are you serious? Were any agents hurt? How's Boudreaux? You didn't get shot, did you?" she asked, concern threading through her voice.

"I'm fine. Boudreaux's fine, and no agents were harmed. They refused to surrender and paid the ultimate price."

"Fuck 'em!" exclaimed Jules.

"Jules Casto Waters, listen to that potty mouth," said Rick with a laugh.

"I know. I don't care. They deserved it. They shot a freaking missile at us!"

"I agree totally. It was swift, final justice. I'm gonna let you go, baby. I'm gonna call the rest of the team and then call Jake and let him know they can come home. Well, home to one though, since his actual home was destroyed. But you know what I mean."

"We should all go out to dinner tonight. Carson, the SWAT team, Boudreaux, all of us, and celebrate. I'll see if I can reserve a private room somewhere," said Jules.

"Great idea. I'll talk to Carson to see if we can make that happen."

"I'm glad you're safe, Rick. I love you."

"I love you too, Jules. See you soon."

Next, Rick called Possum.

"Hey, buddy. It's over. They are all pushing up daisies now."

"For real? Wow. That's insane. I assume they were met with overwhelming force?" Possum replied.

"Damn straight. I'm gonna call Jake and let him know it's safe for him and Cindy to return. I'll let Gary know too," Rick said.

"Awesome. I know there won't be a trial now but I have found some interesting paper trails in all those documents. I'm gonna keep going down the rabbit hole. It may lead to some more arrests."

"Do your thing, hombre. Once this is all wrapped up, Jules and I are gonna come back to Destin and take the motorhome down to the Everglades. I bought a Jeep that can be flat-towed."

"Sweet! I can't wait to see it," Possum responded.

"Alright, buddy. You and Malia take it easy. Say hi to Johnie for me."

Rick hung up and called Jake.

"Jake, it's Rick. It's all over now. Vito and his crew are all dead. There won't be a trail and y'all are safe to return to Apalachicola."

"Oh man. That's so good to hear. Dead huh? What happened?" asked Jake.

"It was like an old west shoot out. But our side had more weapons and better skills. It ended almost as soon as it started."

"Damn. Thanks for the update. I'll tell Cindy. You wanna speak to Gary? He's right here."

"Yeah."

"Hey, Gary. Did you hear any of that?" Rick asked.

"No, but from the look on Jake's face, it sounds like Vito's crew won't be causing trouble anymore."

"Yep, they all paid the ultimate price. Suicide by cop, so to speak. Listen, how quickly can you get to Apalachicola? Jules is putting together a dinner at one of the restaurants for Carson and his crew. Can y'all make it?"

"I don't see why not. The jet is here, and Clay said he can land at the Apalachicola airport instead of Tallahassee. The runway is a little short, but it's okay for the 737. We can leave within the hour."

"Great, see ya soon. I'll text you what restaurant she lines up. She was shooting for 7:00 p.m., so we have plenty of time."

Rick climbed into the SUV with Carson and Boudreaux. He shared the dinner plans with Carson, who thought it was a great idea. He noted that he'd have to report to Washington and could do that over Zoom, but he would round up his team to meet them wherever Jules secured a reservation.

"There will be about twenty of us total," Carson said.

"She'll make it happen. She's amazing," Rick concurred.

After picking up Jules at the safe house, they drove toward Tallahassee to pick up the Jeep. She had arranged to wire the money for Rick, and the salesman had fueled up the Jeep and changed the oil. They just needed to return the rental cars and grab an Uber back to the car lot.

Jules drove the rental car stashed by the bookstore and followed Rick. They were back in a couple of hours, and when they returned, Jules got confirmation of the restaurant she had been working on. They would rent the entire brewery at Eastpoint Beer Company. The owner would provide pizza and craft beer for the entire team. He said he wanted to pay for it. As honorable as that was, Rick knew Gary would donate a large sum of money at the end and make sure the owner, Josh, accepted it.

"I need a shower," said Rick.

"We still have the keys for the original rental Jake put us up in."

"Oh shit! Great idea! Remember that massive shower with the rainforest water showerhead?"

"Trust me, I have plans for you in there, Mr. Waters," she teased.

"I like the way you think, Mrs. Waters."

Crossing the bridge in the Jeep, they parked in the circular driveway, still enjoying plenty of daylight. Decision made, they took two of the motocross bikes from Jake's entry property. Jules was impressively getting good at popping wheelies— something Rick found not at all surprising, as she seemed capable of anything she set her mind to.

They rode out to the area taped off where the young girl's body had been discovered, the scene somber and heavy. After removing their helmets, they held hands and said a prayer, seeking closure for the victims' families in this tragedy.

After a brief ride, they returned to the beach house rental. As the warm water cascaded over their bodies, they felt the stress of the day melt away. They made love under the gentle rain shower and then slipped into bed, tangled together in bliss.

Rick was awakened by a text from Gary. *We have arrived.* It was 5:14 p.m.

Come to the rental house where we had the catamaran.

"Will do! I rented a big van. We can all ride together to dinner in it."

Sweet!

Gary, Kelly, Jake, Cindy, and Clay arrived thirty minutes later. Rick animatedly recounted the entire gun battle scene in the great room while Gary sipped a Busch Light tallboy. He casually mentioned that he had driven by and shown Jake the remnants of his house. He was heavily insured and took the loss in stride. Around 6:20 p.m., the group headed to the brewery, where Boudreaux rode alongside Carson.

As Rick and Jules stepped inside, they were met with a sign on the door reading: *Closed for Private Event.* A standing ovation erupted, punctuated by chants of "Speech, speech!" from the gathered crowd.

Rick waved Boudreaux over. "I want to thank Carson, the FBI, and all of you for your assistance. I'd also like to thank Possum, who is recovering at home in Destin and can't be here. But the man of the hour is not me. It's Boudreaux. He went undercover and took insane risks to gather the intel needed to make this mission successful. I think Boudreaux should say a few words."

Boudreaux grinned and shook Rick's hand. "In my past life, I'd have extreme anxiety around so many lawmen. But thanks to Rick, I have a new life. I'm proud to give back. I feel like I'm on the right side of history. Thank you all. *Laissez les bons temps rouler!*" he hollered, raising his beer. The phrase, translated from French, means "let the good times roll."

Carson stepped forward, shaking Boudreaux's hand with a plaque in his other hand. "On behalf of the FBI, the task force, myself, and the president of the United States, I would like to give the award to Nathan Boudreaux."

Carson handed Boudreaux the award, and he was visibly moved. It was the Louis E. Peters Memorial Award, the highest honor for a civilian, jointly presented by the FBI and the Society of Former Special Agents. Boudreaux thanked everyone and proudly carried his award back to his table. Rick could see his eyes were misty as he stared at it. He had come a long way since breaking legs for the crooked noses at Cajun Connection back in the Big Easy.

"Drink up, everyone!' hollered Gaery as he took a big chug from his Busch Light, which he had brought in. He wasn't into craft beer. He gave Josh, the owner, an envelope and made him promise not to open it. All it said on the front was 'Name A Beer After Me.' Inside was ten thousand dollars.

The laughter, clinking of glasses, and cheers echoed into the wee hours, with pizzas and beer flowing freely. Clay made himself the designated driver, sipping only a few, while Rick indulged in a half-bottle of Buzz Drops. Plans were set for breakfast with Carson the next day at the beach house. Rick wished that Possum could be there to join in the celebrations.

Jake came over with Cindy around 9:30 a.m. He brought fresh lobster and scallops he had picked up from Lynn's Quality Oysters. Rick planned to try his hand at making seafood eggs

Benedict. Carson arrived shortly after Jake and Cindy. The breakfast came out perfectly. Jules made candied praline bacon, which she had learned about in New Orleans, and Boudreaux approved. They all gathered in the great room after breakfast to talk.

"What's your plans now, Jake?" asked Rick.

"Same as before, I suppose. Finish the brew pub and get the brewery going. It will be easier now with all this insurance money. I had extended myself a bit before this, to be honest."

"Really? You seemed to be doing well with the beach house rentals and everything," said Rick, concerned.

"Banks are a motherfucker. They decided one day to call in all my loans at once. Said I was too leveraged. I hate them," Jake admitted, frustration leaking through his words.

"I get that," Rick said, empathizing. "All good though, Rick. You'll get your reward, and I'm back in business again!"

Noticing Jules doing the dishes, Rick wandered over to help. "You didn't have to do this, baby. It could've waited."

"I hate dirty dishes piling up."

"I know," replied Rick.

He was about to set his phone on the kitchen counter when it buzzed. It was a group text from Possum to Rick and Carson. When Rick saw it, his jaw dropped, and he looked over at Carson, who had the same look on his face. He stopped what he was doing, whispered in Jules's ear to follow him to the great room, and sat down beside Carson.

"Jake, out of curiosity, what was inside that envelope from Lloyds of London?"

Jake looked surprised and put off that Rick would ask such a personal question.

"It was just a business payout," he replied, not realizing the implications of his statement.

"So, when did you come up with the plan to have your own daughter kidnapped for insurance?" Rick pressed, his voice low but firm.

All the blood drained from Jake's face, and he turned white. Cindy looked like she had seen a ghost as she looked over at her dad. Jake was silent, and Rick could see the little hamster on the wheel in his head running at full speed.

"I, I, well it's not how it appears. I just..." he said nothing mainly and couldn't come up with an answer fast enough.

He looked defeated.

"You're under arrest for kidnapping and insurance fraud. Stand up, Jake," Carson declared, his tone unforgiving.

"How could you do this, Dad? What if they had killed me?" Cindy cried, her voice trembling.

"It was a business arrangement! I never expected it to get this out of hand," Jake pleaded, desperation in his voice.

"Is this because of all the online gambling you do?" Cindy queried, her brown eyes shimmering with tears.

Jake lowered his head in shame, knowing that he was trapped in a web of his own making. Carson stepped forward, handcuffing Jake and reading him his Miranda rights. Cindy collapsed into a chair, sobbing, as Jules wrapped her arms around her, providing comfort.

None of them had seen this coming. Possum's relentless search for the truth had uncovered irrefutable evidence that Jake had collaborated with Vito to arrange Cindy's kidnapping in exchange for allowing Vito to use his empty property. Rick could only pray that Jake hadn't known Vito was using it to bury bodies, a discovery that would devastate Cindy far more than she was already experiencing.

was. Carson took Jake into custody, and Jules continued to comfort Cindy, who was a mess. She loved her dad and tried to wrap her head around it. She knew he had a gambling problem but didn't know how bad it was. Jake would do time for his crime. How much depended on what lawyer he got, how chill the judge was, and whether he had no knowledge of the property being used as a burial site for murder victims. It took Rick a while to understand why Jake would hire him to find his daughter, but Jake thought Rick would get her released and that would be the end of it. He never accounted for Possum's online detective skills. Jake's happy ending would turn into incarceration.

CHAPTER
TWENTY

Rick and Jules sped back to Destin in the Jeep, excitement coursing through them. Clay had flown Kelly and Jake back in the jet while they hooked the Jeep to their Entegra motorcoach, ready for a much-needed family getaway. Chief and Choco came along for the trip. As they drove south on I-75, Rick caught a radio commercial for the Fort Lauderdale International Boat Show. Feeling adventurous, he diverted their route to take the turnpike down, eager to explore the latest fishing gear. Jules, on the other hand, was excited about the mega yachts on display. The boat show would be a perfect side trip before their adventure in the Everglades.

Jules found them a spot at Yacht Haven Park & Marina, which was only a short drive from the boat show, and they hooked up for a two-night stay. Since they had arrived late, Jules whipped up dinner in the motorhome, and they planned to wake up bright and early to hit the boat show as soon as it opened.

~

"Two tickets, please," Rick said at the entrance.

Once they had their hands stamped, they stepped inside, greeted by the sprawling expanse of the massive boat show. Rick made a beeline for the fishing tent, while Jules wandered off to check out the boats. They agreed to meet later at the cocktail barge by the front entrance.

Rick felt like a kid in a candy store. He eagerly purchased custom handmade baitcasting rods and two brand-new Abu Garcia Zenon MG-X low profile reels to match. After filling his bag with tackle that nearly overflowed, he made his way to the floating cocktail barge. Jules was already seated at a table, enjoying a Diet Coke and watching a musician named Eric Stone play live island music with a repertoire of Bob Marley and Jimmy Buffett songs.

After a while, Rick wandered over to a booth behind the stage where he spotted some mud boots at the Everglades Fishing Company booth. Since they were headed to the Everglades, he wanted to meet the owner and get some insights. He hit it off with Jimmy Wheeler, a longtime Everglades resident who had transformed his charter business into a high-end clothing and fishing line.

"You can't go wrong with my gear, built by a fisherman for fishermen," Jimmy emphasized, showing off his products. Rick stocked up on boots and shorts, and Jimmy even gifted him a free hat.

"Do you know anywhere I can park my motorhome in Everglades City? I've never been," Rick asked.

"Are you self-contained?" Jimmy inquired.

"Yep, we can dry-camp for a few days if necessary."

"Park at my store. You can't miss it; it's on the right as you drive into Everglades City."

"Are you serious?" Rick was astonished.

"Hell yeah. If you wanna get a park after that, you can drive down to Chokoloskee RV Park, just south of Everglades City. It's a sweet little island with a lot of history. When you get to the store, ask for Tim. He's my right-hand man there."

"Wow, thank you, Jimmy. I really appreciate it."

With his new Everglades Fishing Company cap perched on his head, Rick returned to Jules to enjoy the music for a bit longer. They tipped the talented guitarist and made their way back to the Jeep to walk Choco and check on Chief. They planned to leave early the next morning and drive down Highway 41 to Everglades City. While Alligator Alley could get them there faster, Rick preferred the scenic route, knowing Jules would love stopping at the Skunk Ape Research Center along the way.

For dinner that night, they dined at Fogo de Chão, a Brazilian steakhouse famous for unlimited cuts of meat served tableside. Rick was a big fan of buffalo mozzarella but always began with steak selections, ensuring he got his money's worth at the all-you-can-eat establishment. After dinner, Jules rolled Rick back to the Jeep, and they returned to the RV park. Snuggled in the king-size bed, the four of them—Rick, Jules, Chief, and Choco—slept like bugs in a rug.

Jules helped Rick hook up the Jeep to the back of the motorhome, and they left the RV park at sunrise. As they drove south and turned onto Highway 41, Rick pointed out the air plants in the trees along the road. The landscape of the Everglades was unlike anywhere else in Florida. Tall cypress trees draped in long-flowing Spanish moss looked prehistoric, and the alligators and American crocodiles added to the scene. Rick told Jules how invasive the big snakes had become in the area and how people were getting paid to remove them by any means necessary. They stopped at Shark Valley to take the loop on their bikes. Since the government was shut down, they got in for free.

"Bonus!" exclaimed Rick.

The government shutdown saved them forty dollars. Rick took the bicycles off the rack in the back, and they took a counterclockwise route on the loop. Rick pointed out all the gators he saw, and Jules began to see more than he spotted and missed. There were schools of bass in each water area, and Rick wished he had brought his new rod and reel and some artificial worms. It took them a few hours to make the loop with all the photos Jules stopped to take. Rick put the bikes back in the rack and fired up the big Cummins.

"Skunk Ape time!" Rick laughed, excitement building.

They pulled into the Skunk Ape Research Center and took the tour, which proved to be both funny and educational. Some visitors believed the Skunk Ape was just an escaped orangutan from years past, while others insisted it was Florida's answer to Bigfoot.

Once the tour concluded, they continued toward Everglades City. True to Jimmy's words, it was easy to find. Rick pulled in and stepped inside the Everglades Fishing Company.

"Are you Tim?" he asked, looking for help.

"That depends. Are you here to arrest me?"

"Ha-ha. No, I met Jimmy Wheeler, and he told me to ask for you. That's my rig, our front. He said I could park her here for a few nights. Can you show me the best spot so I won't be in the way? I'm Rick Waters, by the way."

"Tim, Timothy Lee Kelley, but my friends just call me Tim. Let me show you where to park."

Tim led Rick to a suitable spot beside the store and gave him a quick rundown of the town and best places to eat.

"Are you his dad?" Rick asked casually.

"Hell no! Jimmy's dad is a mountain of a man compared to me. I work here and fish...mostly fish," Tim replied with a smirk.

"Cool! Where should I go to catch fish?"

"Check with Mike down at the Smallwood Store. He knows these waters better than anyone. The store is a museum too; highly recommend checking it out. You can also ask Jimmy when he gets back from the boat show—he might even take you fishing."

"I thought you liked to fish?"

"I do, but you said catch fish. I don't catch much; I like to fish. By fish, I mean drinking a beer and tossing a bobber in the water," Tim said with a smile.

"Fair enough," Rick chuckled.

Settling in, Rick browsed maps of the area online, eagerly anticipating his chance to dip a line into the Seminole waters. The days ahead promised adventure in the heart of one of Florida's most unique ecosystems.

EPILOGUE

J ake was indicted for kidnapping and eventually pleaded guilty to the charges. He was required to return the Lloyd's of London insurance money, but as part of the plea deal, the charges related to the insurance fraud were dropped. Cindy, showing remarkable compassion, forgave her father and pleaded with the judge for leniency on his behalf. In a turn of events, Jake was ordered to never gamble again, and the judge imposed the mandatory minimum of four years. Given good behavior, he was expected to serve two years before being eligible for parole.

It was determined that Jake had no knowledge of Vito using his land to bury murder victims. Cindy visited her dad every week. With her now at the helm and money not disappearing because of online gambling, the brew pub finally opened.

A total of twenty-one bodies were recovered from the vacant land Jake owned on St. George Island. Jake had Cindy set up the site as a memorial area and vowed never to develop it. They built large granite plaques for each girl who lost her life during his time in prison, Jake focused on turning his life around and deepening his spirituality. He found solace in his faith, hoping to become a better man when he was released.

The brew pub was a huge success, and Cindy created a tour that would visit all the breweries in the area in a van. Instead of completing it, they all worked together to bring the community closer. Josh Parker created a beer and named it after Gary. It had a sketch of a bushmaster snake on the front, and it was called Gary's Buschmaster Brew, and of course, it tasted exactly like a Busch Light. It would only be available in tallboy cans.

THE END

Acknowledgments

I want to thank my beta readers, Mike Keevil and Chris Bowers.

I want to thank my amazing editors, Arly Gramm and Izzy Lily.

Thanks to my graphic artist Les.

Special thanks to Nick Sullivan, Wayne Stinnett and Bob Adamov for all their support and advice over the years.

I want to thank all the readers of my novels, especially. It's all about the readers. I appreciate your continued support on this journey.

ABOUT THE AUTHOR

Eric Chance Stone was born and raised on the Gulf Coast of Southeast Texas. An avid surfer, sailor, scuba diver, fisherman, and treasure hunter, Eric met many bigger-than-life characters on his global adventures. Wanting to travel after college, he got a job with Northwest Airlines and moved to Florida. Shortly after that, he was transferred to Hawaii, then Nashville. After years of being a staff songwriter in Nashville, he released his first album, Songs For Sail, in 1999, a tropically inspired collection of songs. He continued to write songs and tour and eventually landed a gig with Sail America and Show Management to perform at all international boat shows, where his list of characters continued to grow.

He moved to the Virgin Islands in 2007 and became the official entertainer for Pusser's Marina Cay in the BVI. After several years in the Caribbean, his fate for telling stories was sealed.

Upon releasing his 15th CD, All The Rest, he was inspired to become a novelist after meeting with Wayne Stinnett. Wayne, along with Cap Daniels, Chip Bell, and a few others, became his mentors, and they are all good friends now. Eric resides in a 44' Entegra Aspire motorhome with his fiancée Kim-Cara. They live wherever they are parked.

Inspired by the likes of Clive Cussler's Dirk Pitt, Wayne Stinnett's Jesse McDermitt, Cap Daniels' Chase Fulton, Chip Bell's Jake Sullivan, and many more, Eric's tales are sprinkled with Voodoo, Hoodoo, and kinds of weird stuff. From the bayous of Texas to the Voodoo dens of Haiti, his twist of reality will take you for a ride. His main character, Rick Waters, is a down-to-earth, good-ol'-boy and an adventurist-turned-private-eye who uses his treasure-hunting skills and street smarts to solve mysteries.

Also by Eric Chance Stone

Blue Waters

Vanishing Waters

Raging Waters

Back Waters

Muddy Waters

Mayan Waters

African Waters

Deep Waters

Baja Waters

Canuck Waters

Junkanoo Waters

Arctic Waters

Pirate Waters

Dark Waters

Persian Waters

Zombie Waters

Rising Waters

Still Waters

Kona Waters

Emerald Waters

Team Waters

Coming soon - Seminole Waters

www.ingramcontent.com/pod-product-compliance
Lightning Source LLC
Chambersburg PA
CBHW051948220626
47052CB00004B/840